The Other Man

Dangerous Love & Secrets

By

London Starr

Remember....

You haven't read 'til you've read #Royalty

Check us out at www.royaltypublishinghouse.com

#royaltydropsdopebooks

Text ROYALTY to 42828 for sneak peeks and

notifications when they come out!

Chapter One

On a quiet night in Tucson Arizona, a stormy and stimulating rendition of Malachiae Warren's "R U Down" flows through the darkness coating Jané Sullivan's upscale home. Soulful, sensual lyrics are put to an unhurried piece of music and wrap around her trembling shoulders as she lays in her bed alone and crying. The song is giving her the only warm embrace she has felt in a long time. Normally, she would be moaning under her husband's well-built frame as he rocked into her until she came apart in his arms. But tonight she listens in agony as the song describes in raw details exactly what she is lacking; love from the man that is supposed to be down for her. But she cannot turn the tormenting song off; it is the only thing that has touched her in months.

By all rights, she should not feel this low when she is married to an extraordinary breed of man. Quon Sullivan is successful, black, handsome, and has big dreams of bringing his shipping and exporting company to Fortune 500 status. But, his ability to call when he is going to be late changed six months ago. So have a lot of other things about their four year marriage. This is the third night this week that he has not come home before three in the morning. The only thing working at that hour in the corporate world is people in G-strings and six-inch heels.

If Jané had the slightest inkling that Quon would treat her like this, she would have steered clear of him seven years ago when she met him at college. Especially now that she is convinced he is cheating on her.

She tried to deny it at first. Willful ignorance left her with hope that they could get past this. So, she has not checked his phone for strange numbers, sniffed his clothes for foreign fragrances, and rifled through his pockets. Hard evidence of his adultery would have shattered her heart into pieces and filled her head with images of him with other women. She would never be able to forget it. Her hunch about Quon's extracurricular activities is bad enough. Jané just wants to focus on repairing the breakdown of their marriage, not point fingers. She knows the other person receiving his love is not blameless however, just not a thief either. Quon is giving himself away.

What hurts her most is that he vowed that he would stay true to only her in the same church in Atlanta that her parents married in over twenty years ago. He has violated the memories of the time she spent there with them. Those memories are all she has left since they were killed in a car crash just before she went off to college. But she cannot imagine a life without Quon. She needs him more than she needs air to breathe though he has broken her heart. She loves him enough to forgive him for it. She just hopes that when she confronts him, he will go back to being the good man that he used to be.

Now, she watches the clock, waiting for him to return. Quon will have to promise to stop ripping her heart out of her chest. The cheating and the late hours have to go too before she forgives him for anything. Or Jané does not know what she will do. Quon is her life and all the family she has in Arizona besides her best friend, Simone Caslon. Everyone else is back home in Staten, Georgia.

Then, a soft creak from the front door opening downstairs brings Jané out of her grieving for a love she hopes is just gone astray, not gone completely. She listens for Quon's foot falls on the curving staircase leading to the three bedrooms. Two are empty for now. But she wants children desperately, *his* children. Quon does not. He keeps telling her that he needs to make Sullivan's Global Shipping more successful. But, he makes over half a million dollars a year. Two million sits in the bank drawing interest.

How much more money does he need, Jané asks herself just as Quon walks into the bedroom. He does not bother to turn on the light. She watches his silhouette move toward bathroom like clockwork. He will jump right into the shower then stick to his side of the bed by gripping the edge of the mattress like it is a lifeline. Then he will fall asleep quickly without acknowledging her. The first night he did this to her crushed her. She never felt so rejected and unwanted, her heart never so broken.

Acid and anxiety build in her throat as she sits up and reaches for the knob on the crystal lamp that has reflected her misery back to her for one hundred and eighty-three of the loneliest days she has ever spent in this house. Quon stops dead in his tracks halfway between the doorway and the bathroom. The music dies abruptly as if it knows something is about to happen and should pay attention.

Quon's head teeming with closely cropped waves and wide eyes begins to swivel towards Jané, who is eyeballing him from a massive mahogany bed. She knows she looks bad. Her messy ponytail sways to the side of her head like its drunk above baggy pajamas two sizes too big for Jane's slim body. She lost her appetite when she realized her marriage was going downhill on a pair of roller skates without any brakes.

Then, Quon's mouth begins to open and close like a fish before he clears his throat.

"Hey...ah...baby. I didn't mean to wake you."

Jané hears and fears his hesitation before he called her baby. The term of endearment clearly no longer applies to her. The tension in the room ratchets up a notch as he tugs on his tie like it is choking him, making it lay crooked across his wide chest. Her eyes travel slowly down his body to the tails of his white dress shirt. They hang sloppily over his gray slacks with millions of creases in the wrinkle-resistant expensive fabric. His matching jacket is balled in a tight fist and dragging the ground.

Busted, Jané thinks. She has never known Quon to be so rough with anything in his life.

The woman he is sleeping with has to be one powerful lay if Quon is treating his clothes this badly. Or maybe it was not him that was rough with his clothes tonight.

Jané's mind starts to swim with images of another woman's hands tearing at Quon's clothes. Her heart fractures down the middle.

I guess what is beneath his clothes belongs to the other woman now.

She smirks and shakes her head.

"You didn't wake me, Quon. Who is she?" she asks casually as if they are discussing the weather.

His eyes begin to bulge in his face.

"Who is who?" he asks in an unnaturally high tenor then swallows convulsively, guiltily.

Jané closes her eyes, wanting to scream at him for hurting her like this. But she knows reacting like that will only anger him. Then, an argument will follow, and none of their problems will get resolved. So, she takes a deep breath then dwells inside her aching soul for the willpower to keep her emotions in check.

She finally says in a whisper, "The woman that you want more than me, Quon." A ghostly pain scurries through her chest. It hurt to say the words. A sigh escapes him just as the CD player above her head releases the first note to, Teyana Taylor's "Do Not Disturb".

"Baby, that is not what's going on. I swear," Quon says suddenly, making Jané's eyes fly wide open this time.

He is lying.

Jané begins to feel like a fool for wanting to fix anything with someone that will lie to her. She loses a little more control over her emotions, growing closer to screaming at him anyway.

Instead, she takes a harsh breath before saying through gritted teeth, "I'm not stupid, Quon. If you can't be honest with me, we can't fix this problem coming between us."

Quon shifts his weight from one black, suede Italian shoe to the other. The fist that is strangling his coat swings out then returns to his side again.

"There's nothing to fix, Jané. You're being overdramatic."

Anger and desperation slash at Jané's chest. She closes her eyes again, all the while knowing she is getting nowhere with Quon. And unless she can get him to confess, their marriage is headed nowhere, too. Silent tears seep between her long eyelashes. She takes a rattling breath.

"Quon, you're lying as well as staying out all night and cheating on me. I'm willing to forgive you but you have to tell me what it is that I need to forgive," she pleads between fresh surges of unhappiness that are cutting her throat in half. He inhales harshly, drawing her miserable gaze to his. His face scrunches up. She knows that he is in a foul mood now.

"What if I don't want your forgiveness, Jané? What if I like being free to come, go, and sleep with whoever I want to when I get ready?" he asks angrily.

Jané's mind sways sideways, unable to believe that Quon asked her that.

This man cannot love for me if he can treat me this way when I sit here waiting for him to come home every night, she thinks incredulously as her anger grows skyward. *I have no life. Yet, he seems unhappier than me.*

She becomes terrified that she may have to let him go. She cannot hold their marriage together alone. She has always been a realist first, then a clinger.

"Then why did you marry me, Quon?" she whispers as her heart shatters in her chest. Her mind wants to stay wrapped around the illusion that the Quon she married will come back to her. But she senses that he will not now or ever. Still, she holds onto hope that she can convince him to work on their relationship.

Quon slams his empty hand into his powerful thigh and looks heavenward before blowing air into the ceiling fan spinning lazily above them. It does not seem as if he is going to explain why he does not want her anymore. But, he will if Jané has to choke it out of him.

"Why?" she yells, losing it completely.

He looks at her finally.

"Because, Jané, you were beautiful and I loved you," he answers quickly. "I thought life would be perfect with you. It's not."

Perfect! Who can live up to that?

Most people do not even try. But, Jané tried anyway, failed obviously, and is getting a little closer to accepting that this marriage is over, maybe even doomed from the start. Then her mind begins to twist with his words.

He loved me, not loves. I was beautiful, not am. I'm past tense.

"Nothing is perfect, Quon. If you wanted to leave me, why didn't you say it sooner instead of putting me through all this?" Then she begins to cry as her worst nightmare comes true. Quon is gone.

"Because I…" He pauses then stares at her like he wishes he could change what he is about to say, but will not, even for her.

"…I didn't want you to be alone, Jané. Your family is in Georgia. I shouldn't have asked you to quit college so I could come out here and start my business sooner. But I promised to take care of you forever and it wouldn't be right to divorce you and leave you here by yourself." Jané's head becomes light like it wants to float away.

I sacrificed my career for him. Now he does not want me after he becomes successful. How stupid could you have been, Jané?

She begins swiping at the rapidly escaping tears. At least she had an answer to one of her many questions. Quon came home every morning because he pitied her. To Jané, that is worse than being lied to, cheated on, and dragged through his life because he is not the man that she loves anymore. Pity means she is helpless, unable to be a whole person alone, and needs a guardian. But she runs this house like a well-oiled machine solo, and makes friends easily. Well, she thought she did. Wouldn't someone who knows about Quon's affair have told her? How many people know that he has made a fool of her?

Yet, Jané still cannot bring herself to give up completely on her marriage. It is supposed to last forever.

She sets pleading eyes on his angry face.

"Quon, we can fix this. Tell me what you want from me," she appeals from the bed, feeling like she might as well be on her knees begging with her hands out for the last morsel of love inside him, though she cannot figure out what made him stop loving her in the first place.

He begins to shake his head slowly.

"Jané, look at you. You don't dress up anymore or go out. Your life is about me. What do you have without me?"

When he ridicules her for being a good wife and putting her husband and his needs above all others, she descends into shock.

"I had no reason to go anywhere because *you* stopped inviting me out," she hisses. "I didn't know I was baggage to you now. Am I wrong for wanting to be a part of your life? Or am I just in the way of the time that you spend with *her* now?"

He drops his eyes to the floor.

"I'm sorry, Jané. I thought I'd love you for life but I want someone else now and… I want a divorce."

The room begins to spin around Jané. She closes her eyes again to stabilize herself, trying to understand when and why Quon started thinking of her as a weight holding him down, forcing him to steal his happiness from another woman.

"Who is she?" she asks quietly, unable to speak any louder or risk cracking what little self-composure she has left, wide open.

When he says nothing, she gives him a frosty glare while starting to feel numb inside.

"I have the right to know who helped you destroy our marriage, Quon."

He steps back.

"It doesn't matter. You can have the house. It's paid for. I'll give you a generous divorce settlement and alimony. You won't ever have to work. I made that promise and I'm keeping it," he vows softly as if that will make up for all the pain he has caused her.

"It *does* matter. I should know who you will be cheating on next. Yes, I'll take the house since you think I have nowhere to go. Working is the least of my worries. And I'm glad you're keeping at least one of your promises to me," she says scornfully, her tone just as cold as her flesh is growing from being duped, dumped, and about to be ditched.

Damn straight a job does not even count among my troubles right now. I will probably need two therapists to talk me through my new life; one for the lonely days, one for the empty nights.

But Jané has been navigating those already. She just was not if she would make it through them without Quon. She will have to find a way now.

More tears slip silently down her face as she fully accepts that her marriage is done. Her world is crashing down around her and so is the composure she tried so desperately to hold onto.

"Who is she?" she screams suddenly, making Quon flinch slightly.

"Marilyn," he deadpans.

"Marilyn fucking who? Monroe? The state? Does she not have a last name?"

Quon swipes at his face wearily.

"Marilyn Connor. She's being running my advertising department for a year now," he confesses finally.

This is real. The other woman is real. And now a trip to divorce court is real.

If the cliché of husbands cheating with someone in the workplace was not so real, Jané would lose her mind completely. Instead, she reaches for the lamp, turning it off, not able to stand the sight of Quon for another second. She slips down the mattress then folds her body into the fetal position, letting her tears rage out of control as much they want in the dark where no one can see.

For six months, Jané hid the state of her marriage from everyone. She became a hermit when Quon became a ghost, haunting his own home in the early morning hours after leaving the woman that he has been cheating with.

Marilyn wins. I have no more fight left, though I would give my next breath to change Quon's mind about the divorce.

She also cannot help but to think that if she had not said anything about his other life with Marilyn, she would still have a few hours every night with him at least. Gathering the courage to confront him only brought about her world down around her. Now she has nothing. But nothing is better than residing on the outskirts of his life while living *with* him and suffering from unrequited love that he once returned passionately, basically making her a stalker.

How is that even possible? she asks herself.

What will she do with her life now? Where will she go when she gets tired of looking at the same four walls meant for a family?

No answers come forth immediately, making her cry even harder into the pillow that used to belong to Quon. It is all that she has left of him, so she holds onto it tightly.

In the beginning of her slippery slide into the current hell for a home life, she would ask herself why did Quon marry her if his love easily turns on and off like a light switch. It took Jané months to acknowledge that it may never turn back on for her. Now the question that plagues her most is why Quon comes home at all when he does not want to be here with her anymore.

Jané knows that he can have his pick of any woman in the area. He is tall with a wide nose that compliments his black, bedroom eyes and thick lips that knows where to kiss a woman's body until her panties are soaking wet. He has always coerced a reaction from her even when she is not in the mood for lovemaking. His favorite time for sex would be just before or after his meetings at his office. If she tried to push him off, he would start to whine in a deep cadence while forcing responses from her core with a kiss on her neck or slow glide of his hand down the front of her until she is screaming his name. When he started keeping the wrong hours, their sex life went down the drain.

Before then, they never lacked in the bedroom, shower, living room, or kitchen countertop. Quon is a well hung and satisfying lover that rarely goes two whole days without wanting Jané's leg spread wide and taking his massive erection in deep, until six months ago. She knew then that something was not right with their marriage, and became a whiny wife that could not get a reaction from her husband for several reasons. He was too tired to make love, stressed out about work, late for a meeting, hungry, or needed to take a call in another room with the door shut. Suddenly, he stopped asking her to attend business functions with him. He does not send flowers to her just because it is Tuesday anymore. The time they spent apart began to grow until she had to believe that he is cheating. Then, she became stuck in the world of 'what if'.

What if he never comes back? What if he never loves me like he used to again?

So she quit trying to get anything from him three months ago, hoping the old Quon would return, worried that she was not interested in him anymore. But even praying to God and wishing on every shooting star that she saw on clear Arizona nights did not bring him back to her.

Then, the bed dips behind her. Arms encircle her waist and lift her easily into a hard lap. Her hands move automatically around Quon's shoulders, looking for comfort even if it is based on damn pity. At this point for Jané, comfort is comfort. She crushes the front of her body to his chest, knowing she is clinging but cannot help it. Quon is who she is supposed to cling to.

"God, Quon, don't do this to me. You're all I have," she pleads between sobs. He only squeezes her tighter against him, saying without saying that she will not have him much longer no matter how much she begs.

"I'm sorry, Jané. I really am," he whispers into the crown of her head. She lifts it to stare at the man she thought she knew. She did not know he could be so heartless while trying to be kind. His kindness keeps her eyes glued to his. He is still the most beautiful man she has ever seen, even if he is a cheater. Jané has yet to build up immunity to the appeal that oozes from him. It has always called to her like a siren's song from the moment she laid eyes on him, across the campus of Atlanta University on her first day there. Now she is being dashed against the rocks that his deadly appeal has led her blindly to. Since she has nothing without him, she would not care if she did not survive.

Quon's head dips suddenly. His mouth trespasses against hers, fusing their lips together like an airtight seal. Heat rushes Jané's body. She releases a conflicted moan from low in her throat, torn between pulling him close and pushing him away. Both will cause her pain, but it has been so long since he has touched her like this.

Sharp notes to Lisa Fischer's "How Can I Ease the Pain" tune flows through the night air. The words that glide across the haunting harmony begin and punish Jané with a play by play of her life for the last six months with Quon.

In and out
Out and in you go
I feel your fire
Then I lose my self-control
If it's not love you're coming for
Tell me baby why you're here
Knocking at my door

Quon's tongue enters Jané's mouth, blistering it with the same fire that keeps her soul and body tuned to his channel of love. She should not want to listen to it anymore but desire dampens the space between her thighs, making her pull Quon even closer until there is no air between them.

As his hands glide up the front of her like old times, Jané asks herself how she can be so stupid to still love him when he does not love her back. Shouldn't she be praying for the strength to stay away from him?

But, she does not want to stay away. She figures that she will need all the memories she can get to keep her warm at night when this last time with him is over.

Chapter Two

Phantom hands begin pulling at the buttons of her of shirt, make short work of them, and spread her top open. Quon bares her breasts then slings her sideways, dropping her to the bed on her back. He stands up then bends over her and run his fingertips from the top of her neck to the area between her naked mounds, all the way down to her navel. Jané sucks in air loudly as tiny sparks from his traipsing hand dance along her skin. She loves this betrayer so much still.

Quon chuckles in the dark.

"Still sensitive everywhere, huh?" he asks in a husky murmur that has just as much effect on her as the skin-to-skin contact between them does. But, Jané does not answer. Instead, she begins to wonder does he do this to Marilyn and vice versa, tormenting herself.

Suddenly, Jané's pants are being tugged down her curvy, slim hips, dragging her out of the hellish thoughts beginning to take hold of her mind. Once her pants sail away, she is back in possession of the situation at hand, well aware of Quon kissing the tops of her thighs, and that he lost his clothes while she was thinking. She hisses when a surge of sensation swamps her moistening center and raises her legs to seek relief. She presses her heels into the thick pillow top of the mattress and scoots backwards, seeking even more relief. It seems that going along time without Quon has made her body *too* sensitive to his touch. Then his hands reach out like snakes striking and seize her trembling thighs, pull her right back to where she was, and hold her in one place. When he is sure she cannot move, he squats before her then blows on the wet folds he has not paid any attention to in months, and probably will not ever again after tonight.

Jané decides to milk the situation for all it is worth, becoming very glad that she had not put on underwear after her shower. Quon is still her husband, so she will not be doing anything wrong if she sleeps with him.

Who knows how long it will take to get a divorce or when I will be with another man again? I don't think I can love anyone else like this. I don't want to either.

Right then, she decides she does not want to be with another man, not if she will be treated like this for giving him her heart. This last time with Quon will have to carry her through the days it will take her to build a life without him and repair her heart.

Quon leans forward and tongues her sex, lapping at the juices leaking from her core. It throbs beneath his mouth, needing to be made love to right now. Hopefully, their time together will erase the last lonely six months. Quon's expertise in the bedroom should be able to replace those ugly memories, or at least he was able to before his affair happened. Then, she remembers that Quon is no longer hers.

If I sleep with him now, won't that me make me the other woman?

Jané smirks to herself and mulls over the irony of having to grant Quon a divorce to get him to touch her.

No wonder some women prefer to be the side piece. They get all the fun a man can be and none of the heartache he can cause. There is no pressure on either one to be something they are not to the other; trustworthy and faithful.

Quon sucks at the nub veiled between Jané's thighs, making piercing points of lightning streak through her. She gives a low moan and puts her head back in the game of making a Quon a two-timing cheat with his own wife and another lasting memory for herself.

Hmmm...I think I should give him one or three memories to take back with him, too.

Jané thinks it is a damn fine idea to let *him* remember the things she will do to him while he is screwing Marilyn's brains out at his office desk, on their couch, and in their kitchen. She is sure that Marilyn is most certainly in his thoughts when he comes home, or rather here since this place hasn't been home for either of them lately. It makes her determined to burn memories of her touch in his head before she sends him right back to Marilyn.

She pushes Quon's hands away, sits up then slides up the bed, leaving his mouth gaping wide open over nothing.

Then he groans, "Where are you going, Jané?"

"Get on the bed, Quon," she demands while reaching up to pull the elastic band from her ponytail, letting her thick pencil-straight mane fall down around her shoulders.

"What? Why?" he asks cagily, probably afraid Jané has a knife hidden somewhere, waiting to cut off his double-crossing man parts. She did not. She thinks she probably should whack them off.

But she will not. Those same parts will betray Marilyn one day, the one who will deserve it. But first, Jané wants to give Quon's man parts unforgettable joy for the last time. Then she will do the unthinkable: move on with her life somehow. In time, she will forgive Quon and Marilyn. Her heart does not hold grudges. Life is too short for that. Just ask her parents.

Why should I use precious energy to be angry with them when Karma is an unforgiving bitch that will make them pay for breaking my heart?

She vows to give Quon seven different heavens to travel through before he moves forward with his life. But nothing that has been built on the fractured foundation of another's heartache will do well. Jané would not be surprised if Marilyn and Quon are over before the ink dries on the divorce decree, or maybe they will not be. But she takes comfort in the fact that they will carry the same destructive behavior that ruined her home into their new one, and it will take them both down. *That* she is sure of from the Lifetime movies she has been watching back to back.

Quon glides up the bed to sit beside her as she leans over to turn on the lamp. She does not just want to hear him while she guides him to paradise. She wants to actually see him go.

The bright light sheds generous illumination onto the hard planes of Quon's gorgeous body as he lies down on his back. His impressive manhood juts into the air. The steel casing surrounding it is the color of unpolluted coffee. Jané ogles it, wondering why she has never taken it into her mouth or why Quon has never asked her to. But she will tonight because she has always *wanted* to.

She slips off the bed to a crouching pose before him and drops her hands on his firm thighs outlined in a dizzying array of sculptured muscles. Her mouth waters. Quon shifts to get up as if he does not trust her anywhere near his family jewels.

Yeah, he probably shouldn't, she thinks with a sardonic smile before planting both hands in his midsection and pushing him back down. She dips her head before he tries to rise again and takes the foreign tip of him into her mouth. Her sex contracts like she has taken him inside her body.

Well, I have in a way, she rationalizes before applying pressure like she is sucking on a lollipop.

Quon groans and as she begins to feast on him, feeding more inches of him slowly to herself. His hips start to piston upwards in a slow rhythm of up… then down… up again, giving her more than her mouth can take. He is practically screwing it, causing her center to throb jealously. Jané glances up at Quon. She becomes more than satisfied when she sees he is watching her, too. The look between them quickly becomes the most erotic thing her system has ever been subjected to. So much so, she slides her hand down her front until it is caressing the wet folds shielding the pulsing between her wet thighs. Jané takes much satisfaction in knowing that he is watching closely for every move she makes.

While she has his attention, she seizes the opportunity to pull one of the fantasies from the 'she never told him about it and he never asked' file cabinet in her mind. Usually she puts it back quietly after imagining Quon fulfilling the desires she keeps secret. Now, she is so glad that the time for making those fantasies real has finally arrived, and it could not have come sooner for her.

Her invasive fingers hit a hot spot inside her. She closes her eyes and hums her pleasure around Quon's length that is thrusting in and out of her mouth to the erotic beat of Summerella's "Something". If Jané has her way, everything under the sun will take place in this room tonight.

Quon's hips lose the steady pace he created by plunging in and out of her lips. He tries to sink into the bed. Jané knows the vibrating of her mouth has scattered his senses and he is desperate to run away with them. She cannot let that happen yet, so she dunks her head and swallows more of him until his tip bumps the back of her throat, leaving her with a handful and a half of his base to wrap her tongue around.

"Fuck, Jané!" he hisses then finds a faster, jerkier rhythm again, keeping time to nothing but his body demands for gratification.

At least he didn't call me Marilyn.

Jané would not have been able to handle it if he did. But she is surprised that he even remembers her name. When she is done with him, she will be etched on his mind from now on.

She continues to hold Quon hostage in her throat and slips her fingers in and out of her sticky tunnel begging for him to fill it like he is doing her mouth. Just the thought of him cramming her body to capacity with his rock hard pole makes Jané's core spasm. Her eyes roll back in her head. Her body starts heating up, feeling like she is boiling within. She senses that if Quon continues to pump between her lips, her body will mistake the movements for his cock moving inside the same canal that her fingers are working, and make her explode without him ever touching her. Jané wants to make that happen badly. So she lifts her head until Quon only touches her lips. Then she tries to consume the entire length of him.

Her thumb begins working her clit in short circles while her fingers abuse her hidden walls deliciously. More pleasure than she has ever experienced at anyone's hands bounds through her core. She squeals quietly around Quon. Her fingertips begin to work faster along with Quon's hips thrusting quicker and harder. The combination of their movements takes her over the edge just like she knew it would.

Her eyes rocket open and encounter his burning observation. It only adds more pressure to the currents hurdling through her. Suddenly, Jané needs to scream. She begins to lift her head to do just that when Quon's hands reach and push her head right back down, forcing her to accept him between her tonsils. He fingers press on her scalp, keeping her locked in position.

His thick manhood pulses on her tongue. Her orgasm spikes again. She begins to cum even harder all because her control has been taken away. She loves it, wants more of it, but her knees are buckling beneath her. She moans around the appendage cutting off more than just her speech, indicating she needs to get up now. Quon sinks deeper into her throat instead. His head starts to rock from side to side against the bed as hot spurts of liquid heaven enter Jané's mouth for the first time ever. She swallows before she chokes on her moans trying to escape and his salty essence trying to gain entrance. Nothing has ever tasted so good to her than Quon's pleasure.

His hands fall away to ball in the sheet above his head as his hips rise off the bed. Every single muscle in his body congeals, as he begins to shake uncontrollably beneath Jané. Her body simmers down just in time for her to catch him at his most vulnerable. If Jané was the average woman, she would take advantage and hurt him beyond repair in the place that did the same to her. But she knows his turn for pain will come in time and wants no part of the backlash that will find her if she seizes the opportunity. She has had enough of vicious circles.

She begins to work him hard and enthusiastically instead, tormenting his hellishly sensitive penis with a deep throat, licks, and tight jaws that encase him too snuggly, milking his rod for whatever is left inside it.

Quon shudders and shouts, "Oh my fuck, Jané!"

She is certain the neighbors only yards away, with just a fence of shrubbery to divide their properties on either side, can hear him. She does not care. It seems to turn her feverish body on even more. Quon starts to squirm beneath her then grasps her head with both long-fingered hands tightly. Jané revels in him being torn between pushing her away and pummeling her mouth with more of his stiff erection that is beginning to soften. She waits patiently for him to make up his mind. It only takes a few seconds before he is spearing through her mouth again, colliding with the back of her throat, and hardening again.

"Yes, baby, take all of me," he groans and begins to drive between her lips, making love to her mouth once more. Jané observes him gazing wondrously at his penis, vanishing into her and reappearing like a splendid magic trick that he cannot get enough of. She swirls her tongue around his invading base. Her center ripples again. She realizes she could actually climax again, so she feeds her inner walls her fingers again. Her body responds by rising to the occasion. Soon she will be tipping over the edge into an orgasmic haze, except Quon pushes her head up until his length falls against his rock hard abs. However, Jané stills need satisfaction and she has already figured out she can get it for herself.

She stands up, still working her body with marauding fingers while gazing down at Quon's toned physique. She backs away to get a full view of the body that she loves like it is her very own. More heat pours through her, signaling her approaching climax is speeding up on its way to her just from looking at him.

He is such a beautiful, treacherous man, she thinks to herself. But her body could not care less about the last adjective describing him right now. It is too far gone up the cliff leading to the paradise he just left, and Jané would rather go there instead.

Quon sits up and glides to the edge of the bed then crooks a long finger, beckoning her to him. Jané removes her hand and walks over to him without delay then stands in place, not sure what she is waiting for.

"Straddle me," he commands quietly. She tosses a knee on each side of him slowly then hovers over the wide missile swaying with her movements, like its honing in on her channel that she is already dipping her fingers back into.

Quon's eyes harden.

"Fuck me, Jané. Now," he demands harshly. She smiles faintly; secretly loving being told what to do and that tonight will not be for ordinary missionary.

"Yes, daddy," she whispers coyly. But there is nothing shy about her. She is looking him straight in the eyes, and sorry that they have never played these games in the bedroom before. Making love has risen to a whole other level between them.

Too bad Quon wants someone else now, Jané muses while she chokes a little on the paradox. But right now he wants her and he will have her until she is satisfied and spent as usual.

Jané empties her body of her sticky appendages only to grip the bottom of Quon's shaft, guiding the tip to the entrance that will connect their bodies. She sinks downward until she is sitting fully in his lap then rises until he only occupies the doorway of her sheath. She rocks slowly on the edge of his swollen member then squeezes her muscles tight before forcing him fully inside her again. She experiences every inch of him gliding against her drenched walls and erogenous zones on her down shift. They both moan in harmony.

"Dammit, Jané, you're killing me," Quon whispers gutturally.

Jané giggles softly.

"Good, daddy, now be a good boy and hush. I'm working here."

She rises again. Quon's hands capture her hips as his breathing becomes wrecked and holds her in place, perching over him. He looks up at her with a wide grin.

"Did I say you could talk, woman?"

When she answers with only a smile of her own, his fingers press into her flesh where he holds her firmly, demanding a reply. Tiny bites that are easily ignorable at any other time flutter through her hyperaware flesh now, zoning in on her sex that confuses the pain with pleasure and begins contracting and releasing frenziedly, taking her breath away.

"No, daddy," she murmurs while going quietly out of her mind from the bliss erupting within.

"Now what are you going to do about it?" she goads on the first note of Adrian Marcel's "Spending the Night Alone" leaving the radio mounted in the wall above the bed. Then Jané makes her body inhale Quon again slowly. He jerks beneath her.

"Shit, Jané! What do you think I should do to you?" he gasps. But she is not sure what a suitable punishment would be and suddenly has doubts about getting into this type of play with him. On the verge of separating forever just might be the wrong time to cross this boundary in their sex life. It takes Jané no time at all to blame

Quon for his lousy timing, but she decides to take advantage of something and someone for the first time in her life anyway. And she will like it while doing it.

She leans forward to whisper in Quon's ear, "You could spank my ass, daddy, or better yet..." She waits a beat as another fantasy materializes in her mind. "...fuck me there," she suggests casually. Quon's air rushes out of his mouth, fanning her hair from her face. Jané sits back down in his lap, taking him in to the hilt.

"Or not," she adds nonchalantly like she had not just offered to cater to almost every man's dream.

"Get on your knees, Jané," Quon finally speaks hoarsely.

Jané looks around the room with ample places for him to take her doggy style then back at Quon.

"Where, daddy?"

"On the bed."

She shrugs. "Okay." Then she crawls off his lap onto all fours in the middle of the bunched covers. Quon stands up and vanishes into the bedroom. Jané begins to straighten the yellow, white, and blue Dolce & Gabana bed set like she is not about to indulge in taboo sex and has all the time in the world. And she does. She recognizes that being free even when she does not want to be can have its advantages. She can do all the things she wanted to but thought would make Quon look at her differently, disgustingly. She feels a bit dizzy about being free to have sex the way she really wants; nasty, kinky, dirty, the side to her that she has always suppressed.

Normally, she lets Quon take the lead in the bedroom. He satisfies her no doubt but she has always wanted to try other things most people looked down upon, in public anyway. Now there are unlimited possibilities for a future of getting what she really wants from a man in private. Yet she is frightened of it. Who will hold her down after a bad day and tell her things will be okay, then surround her with strong arms capable of protecting her from the world when it is cruel and cold. It is terrifying that Quon will no longer be her anchor and shelter.

She could call Simone, but that would not be right. Jané has barely talked to her once a week since Quon changed, trying to keep from giving away clues of their troubled home. She will not dump her woes on Simone now either. Jané vows to navigate the latest mine field that Quon has dumped her in the middle of alone, while he thinks he will be free in the perimeters of another relationship with boundaries. She starts to feel an odd elation that she can come and go without answering to anyone or worry about their thoughts of her now. Then Quon's presence fills up the bedroom again.

Jané looks back and discovers a bottle of lotion in his hand. She begins to think that he has probably done this before, maybe even tonight while she waited with a breaking heart for him to return. It should turn her off but she would rather he guide her through this new adventure so she can do it well with another man. And Jané knows she will. She promises to herself to take this time she did not ask for to fulfill every sexual fantasy she has ever had but was too chicken to ask Quon to participate in.

She turns back around and grabs a remote off the nightstand, switches the song playing quietly above her to Lauryn Hill's "Ex-factor". Neither is this thought provoking songstress' lyrics lost on her either. Loving Quon for the last six months has been a battle all because he cannot *nor* will ever be there for her when she needs him again, leaving Jané with scars on the inside she does not think will ever heal.

Still she hopes that he hears the meaning in the song, too. But even if he does not, Jané will still take what he has to give for tonight only, make him scream her name, and pray he cannot stay afterwards. She does not want to be around the man that has hurt her more than anyone else ever has, a moment longer. If Jané has her way, no one will ever hurt her again. Then the tune tells her exactly what she has to do to make sure the last months never repeat themselves; let Quon leave from her heart as well as her life, and she will when they finish linking as lovers or at least work on it.

She drops her elbows to the bed, making the raised globes of her behind spread open, inviting Quon inside them to finish being her first in almost everything she ever imagined they would do in this very bedroom together. The irony of their first time being their last smacks her in the chest dead center and takes a little of the air from her lungs.

Dammit, Jané, this is not the time to get emotional. Concentrate.

Quon is a superb lover if he is nothing else, and Jané knows instinctively that he will not disappoint this time either.

"Beautiful," he utters under his breath. Jané wiggles her ass saucily.

That's right, daddy. That stock of the inventory you're throwing out with the trash, she gloats silently.

Then she plants the side of her face and a small grin on the coverlet, and whispers, "Now, fuck me, daddy, however you want."

The bed bows immediately under Quon's weight. Cold lotion drops onto her backside, slithering between her heated cheeks coasting in the air. The conflicting temperatures force a low ragged moan from her. Her center pulses, begging to be filled. It has always craved Quon's body even when Jané does not. She grudgingly admits to herself that it will probably never change.

"Open your legs wide, baby. I'm a big boy," Quon says cockily.

"Yes you are," she co-signs with a snicker then does as told.

Six feet three inches holds up two hundred pounds of pure fickle man, traitorous toned muscle, and ten and a half inches of thick double-dealing manhood beautifully. Jané promises to not forget this, even though she has no idea of how to *not* yearn for her first lust and first real love.

A slight caress around the forbidden ring of muscles concealed between the globes of Jané's behind snatches her out of her thoughts. An alien but pleasant feeling rocks through her and ratchets up the rippling in her core. She whimpers into the bed. Quon's finger continues to do figure eights, torturing her until she needs to cum again, hard. Her fingers jet to the soaked lips between her thighs that are littered with lotion dripping off her backside. Pleasure echoes quietly through her. Her low purrs give it a voice. Her back arches under the pressure building inside her, readying her body to shoot for the heavens without wings.

Quon chuckles behind her.

"I think you're having more fun without me, Jané," he says good-naturedly, something he has not been in quite a while. Then a blunt object pushes at the illicit zone of her body.

About damn time, she spews in her mind then pushes back until he has barely entered her and a slight burning chases her movement. So does an unexpected surge of blissful undulations through her empty tunnel. Jané suffers a full body shiver, as her body tricks itself into believing Quon has filled her center to capacity and prepares to erupt to reward itself for the deceit. She sails close to the horizon of an orgasm. He gains another inch inside her, hitting a pocket of nerves that begin to sing their thanks through Jané.

"Oh God," she gasps loudly.

Quon freezes.

"Did I hurt you, sweetheart?" he asks worriedly. He has always been a tender lover, knowing his massive girth could do damage.

Jané rocks her head against the bed vigorously.

"God no! Don't stop," she hisses loudly. Quon withdraws then thrusts forward slowly, acquiring more space and adding more fuel to the fire already blazing out of control inside her. She nearly screams her approval but settles for driving her hips backwards, taking him further inside.

He grunts, "What the hell are you doing to me, Jané?"

"Fucking you, daddy. Now make me cum, right now," she demands hoarsely and receives a gentle slap on the rear from Quon's hand. The love tap ricochets softly through her. But Jané is not interested in soft.

"Harder," she requests into the mattress. A much less tender smack assails her backside. Her sex clenches agonizingly. She shrieks and propels backwards until Quon impales her fully. He bellows in surprise. She screams as her body begins to produce cataclysmic and punishing waves of joy in places meant and *not* meant to take a man inside. Jané never thought in her wildest fantasies that a double orgasm was possible or that she could cum this hard.

"Oh my God," she wails and begins to rock back and forth, trying to find some way to endure the flux of ecstasy assaulting every wall in her body. Her turbulent movements cause Quon to slide in and out of her, piercing the storm of her orgasm. It begins to reverberate harder through her as if it got upset that they interrupted the rhythmic flow of too much pleasure. Jané only rocks faster as she tumbles uncoordinated through clouds in a carnal sky.

"Fuck, Jané," Quon bellows suddenly then withdraws from the back door of her body to slam into her entrance constructed for this kind of intimacy. He starts to pound every inch of silken pipe that she can take into her, making her journey into orgasmic rapture endless. But only so much pleasure can be endured before it becomes too much, and Jané has already hit her limit. Quon's thighs colliding with the back of hers like a runaway train seem to aggravate the climax even more. He would push her completely off the bed if his hands were not gripping her hips so tightly, holding her in place.

She begins to chant through the heavenly torment, "OhmyGod! OhmyGod! OhmyGod!" But chanting is *not* helping.

"God, Quon. I can't stop cumming. Let me go," she begs. He tightens his grip and begins to imitate a jackrabbit instead, giving her rush after rush of agonizing thrill on top of the climax working overtime.

"If you think I'm coming out of you anytime soon, Jané, you've lost your mind. I have wanted to fuck you like this for seven years. Now take this wood like a good girl," he commands.

"Why didn't you?" she moans the question between breathless pants.

"I didn't think you were into any of this. And I didn't want to hurt you."

And getting your jollies somewhere else wouldn't?

But Jané keeps the patronizing reply to herself and struggles through fading ripples fluttering in her core to say instead, "I didn't...*Oh God*...think you were either."

Jané comes down off her orgasmic high finally, but she does not know how much more she can take of Quon's body hammering hers. She is hypersensitive to his every stroke and never thought for a second that she could reach this level of carnal enjoyment even with him. If it had not been for lack of communication in their marriage, she is positive she would have way before now, but she did not want him to think she was slutty or aggressive. Apparently this is what he has been wanting all along. She vows to never keep her fantasies to herself again.

But I'll have to fulfill them with someone else without the benefit of a relationship. I'm not letting anyone else hurt me.

For now, she will enjoy every avenue her soon to be ex-husband takes her down, and allow other fantasies to come to the surface of her mind. Talking dirty is one of them.

"Cum in me, Quon, like you did my mouth," she whispers, still somewhat shy about letting the wanton inside her out to play.

"Oh I am, baby. Believe that," he promises in a hushed tone. Jané feels when he thickens inside her almost instantly. She grins behind the sheen of hair covering her face resting sideways on the bed, knowing he is close to tipping over the edge. She tightens the walls of muscles he fits almost too snugly in as a willing prisoner. He groans and digs his fingertips in her hips. His rhythm falters just before he pushes so far inside Jané she can feel when his release begins filling her up and leaking around the lock of their bodies. She starts to roll her hips to worsen his orgasm as payback.

"Dammit, sweetheart, I can't take it," he hisses just like she knew he would, though the pet names that have been spewing from his mouth since they started this fuck fest *is* a surprise. But Jané knows better than to read anything into them. He still cheated, wants a divorce, and is not hers anymore but Marilyn's, who he has already cheated on with his wife. Quon is loyal to no one and Jané refuses to stay with a man like that no matter how much she loves him. However, she can sleep with him. She is a human with needs and it is like Quon's body is made just to meet them.

Well, he's done that and now it's time for us both to go somewhere other than this bed.

Jané stops rotating her bottom suddenly and drives a knee forward with a goal of moving away. Quon's fingers dig into her hips again, stopping all advancement.

"Where are you going, baby?" he asks, obviously surprised at her intended getaway. Usually she would cuddle with him until they both fell asleep. But, she is determined to start as he meant for her to go on, alone, no matter how much it hurts.

She wiggles in his grasp until his hands fall away then she crawls away with Quon's essence gliding leisurely down her inner thigh. She stands beside the bed to smile back at him kneeling on it.

"*I* am going to take a shower. *You* can do the same afterwards or pack your shit and leave now… but remember to *leave,*" she insists smugly.

Quon's thick lips fall open as his eyes widen.

"Jané, we just made love," he bellows as his arms spread as wide as his eyes.

She lifts one finger in the air and wags it at him.

"No, we *screwed*, Quon. I made love to the man that I love. I don't know *you*. But I enjoyed the hell out of Marilyn's man. I wouldn't tell her that by the way when you're walking into her house at…" Jané trails off to lean over and get a quick look at the clock on the nightstand displaying 5:02 in the morning proudly. She straightens up.

"…Five in the morning. But I will give you this piece of advice, Quon. Do to Marilyn what you just did to me and she'll forgive you. I *promise*," she adds haughtily.

"This is my house too, Jané! I still live here," he shouts suddenly, losing his entire cool.

She shakes her head.

"No, you don't. You just told me it was mine to live in it *without* you, remember? Now you can keep your promise or I can fight you in court for it and air all of your dirty laundry to a judge that will probably give me half of your company. But that will take time and since we have no kids, you can be rid of me in thirty days legally with no contest. You wanted Marilyn. Now go be with her." Her tone is so nonchalant even Jané has a hard time believing it is her talking after all she has been put through tonight. But she is not interested in things getting anymore harder or emotional between her and Quon.

"So it's like that? You can just push me away like that," he roars again, making her laugh at his emotional flare-ups when he was so cold earlier while asking her for a divorce.

Oh my, how far the mighty fall when the tables have turned.

"Oh *now* you want me to fight for you, Quon?" she asks on a giggle. "You didn't want that either, remember? And yes I *was* prepared to fight for us. I couldn't imagine a life without you. I even denied my fantasies of making love to you in every way possible and dealt with everything you put me through to keep you. But you don't want to be held onto or want to hold onto me. Now you don't have me. You should be happy." She cannot understand why he is not when he is getting what he wants.

"Well I'm not happy! I didn't know you wanted to try other things sexually!" he continues to shout while dropping his fists to his sides.

She begins to glare at the spoiled, selfish man before her.

"Well you better learn to be happy with *Marilyn* and you can forget about what we just did too."

She smiles arrogantly. "But I know you *won't* and I want you gone after I get out of the shower."

Then she loses the smile and twists her head in true ticked off black woman fashion before saying, "*We're done*, Quon." Her voice is cold and hard and she knows he is not use to this.

Jané would gush over her husband every chance she got. Now she is the one with shocking demands and giving hurtful revelations. She wallows in the new, stronger her that he made possible in only a couple of hours after tearing her to pieces. She guesses time does make a difference when someone needs to toughen up, though her wounds on her heart are nowhere near close to healing. But her will to get through and over this breakup has strengthened tremendously. She recognizes she is learning the hard way that it is okay to let go of people that hurt her time and time again no matter how terrified she is of being alone.

God, I could have gone my whole life loving and waiting for Quon, she thinks sorrowfully. But he moved on while not caring how she would feel about it or appreciating anything she did for his creature comforts. Now, Jané knows that he did not deserve her or anything that she did for him.

"So you used me," he shrieks in an unmanly pitch.

She lift a finger to tap her lips as if lost in thought.

"Not at first, Quon, but it quickly turned into that and you were even better in bed than I ever imagined. I thought sex didn't get any better than being with you and then you topped your damn self," she smirks and wobbles her head. "That was amazing what we just did by the way. You should be proud of yourself. *But…* don't tell Marilyn about it," she mocks then laughs out loud at her own black humor.

"So you're just going to tell me to leave?"

She huffs, tired of the conversation and going in circles with him.

"Isn't that what you wanted? You kicked my ass to the curb because you obviously found something better in Marilyn. Well now I'm on the curb waving goodbye to you. The pressure is off, Quon. Now go. Leave me behind again. I'm fine with it," she hisses.

"No, you're not fine, Jané! You're trying to hurt me!"

She walks around the bed, moving towards the bathroom resolved to be through with this dialogue once and for all.

"The only one that causes pain around here is *you*, Quon. Marilyn could not get from you what you weren't willing to give and now you've cheated on her too. You can't get mad because you're getting what you want: a way *out*."

She stops in the bathroom doorway, flips the light switch on, and looks back over her shoulder.

"Now take the out, stop yelling, and start packing. I'll have a lawyer contact you soon."

Then she slams the bathroom door close and locks it.

Chapter Three

In the shower, thoughts connected to different emotions whirl in her head that she has submerged under a cascade of hot water. She does not know if she wants to cry for her failed marriage to a disloyal prick or scream because she is not sure how to go on without him though she knows she must. Then there are the fantasies fulfilled with the prick that she wants to laugh out loud about. Quon lit a fire to her insides that burned hotter than the sun tonight. But her joy does not last long either, when she realizes that everyone needs to be informed about the split between her and Quon, and why.

Acute anxiety develops from just thinking about baring her soul and losing valued relationships that she has formed with Quon's parents. Of course they will rally to his side. He is their son. But they had become surrogate parents for Jané's deceased ones, and Matilda and Ross Sullivan love her like she is one of their own. Quon's betrayal will sever those ties and Jané will be without parental support again.

She steels herself to hold her head high and face them all along with whatever consequences that follows. She cannot avoid them, and has done nothing wrong but love the wrong man completely. If they cut her off, it will be their loss.

Let's see if Marilyn will bend her corporate knees to help Matilda garden in Atlanta, or get her hands dirty while passing Ross greasy tools when he changes the oil in his and Matilda's cars.

Jané highly doubts if Marilyn can even relate to the down-to-earth middle class people Quon's parents are at heart. They live in a luxurious home he bought them as soon as his company put its first million in his account. Jané instantly liked the couple in their fifties when she met them for dinner a month after meeting their son. It did not take many visits for her to grow attached and love them like they were her parents. She sometimes worries about how quickly she forms attachments since her parents died but that is a problem she will have to be concerned about another day.

Right now, she needs to deal with the Sullivan's son and his reattaching issues. Just how much he is stripping from her with his affair will manifest itself soon. Jané does not think Quon cares about how much more she will be losing either. It is enough to make her hate him. But she will not. Her mind knows nothing lasts forever, no matter how much her heart wishes it would, and Quon will eventually pay for his adulterous ways. Until then, she refuses to give him any more control over her emotions while she waits for it to happen. She is more concerned about her own future, which she will get right on in the morning, only a few minutes away.

After performing the same routine she did earlier before bed, Jané exits the bathroom. She finds the bedroom empty and the usual quiet when Quon is not here, except she is not sure that he is gone. She moves quickly across the room to the dresser on the opposite side and stands beside a huge bay window. It showcases a fat moon surrounded by twinkling stars that will laze about the sky for another hour. She sees none of it as she grabs for the first article of clothing in her nightwear drawer that her hand touches, a black sheer nightie meant to seduce Quon.

Seduction is the last thing on her mind, as she hauls the gown over her wet head before retracing her steps then veering off to the double-sided closet between the bed and bathroom. She walks to the back wall and grabs a wide-tooth comb off her vanity set, a gift from Quon when they moved in. She starts to untangle her mid-back length hair absentmindedly.

For the first time, she feels the urge to snoop through Quon's things. She still does not want hard evidence that he is cheating, just the confirmation that he is gone. She scans the space half the size of the bedroom, looking for what is absent. Only a handful of his suits that she had dry-cleaned earlier this week come up missing. If she did not know to look for them, she would not have thought anything on Quon's side of the closet, neatly crowded with designer professional gear, was moved. Jané thinks it is a joke that he wants to appear professional at all times in public while making a mess of his life behind closed doors.

Just as she decides to exit the room and rifle through his chest of drawers on the other side of the window in the bedroom, she hears, "Yeah, I've packed a bag and leaving like you wanted." Quon has snuck up on her, and scares the shit out of her.

Jané twirls around wide-eyed with her heart beating a mile a minute in her chest, shocked that he is still here.

"Ah...I thought that you had left already actually," she stammers and presses a trembling hand over her nipples straining through the thin material of her gown.

Quon's feet once again wearing loafers bring him forward until he towers over her.

"No I haven't left because you were locked in the bathroom with my products," he sneers with a harsh smirk.

She takes her hand from her chest and waves it dismissively in his face.

"Well it's free now."

He frowns like he is missing something and roves his eyes over Jané's front.

"Why are you dressed like this? Is your boyfriend coming over? Am I *not* leaving fast enough for you?"

She begins to giggle until it turns into peals of loud laughter, unable to believe that Quon is actually angry that she is doing what he hoped she would, move on and get a life. A sheen of water developing from her hilarity, and quickly growing out of control, gathers in her eyes. She swipes at them before actual tears can form while observing Quon glaring down at her. She is pretty sure that a full minute passes before she can get a handle on her mirth.

"Do you really care, Quon? And if I had any sense I *would* have found a boyfriend the first time you stayed out until three in the morning. But I loved you too much to ever hurt you like you that. Now whoever comes to see me and whatever I wear is none of your business. But your shit in my bathroom is your business so go get it and go home," she says highly amused, feeling better and better about him leaving.

He has not even left yet and he is already miserable.

It will only get worse when he is in the next binding relationship. It probably would have killed Jané dead on the spot if she thought for one second he was actually going to be happy when he went back to Marilyn. Unfortunately for Jané, Quon is not moving period.

She stares back for another few seconds then widens her eyes before saying, "Well! What are you waiting for? *Go* get your stuff then *go*. I'll pack the rest of your things and have it shipped to your office. You can tell the moving men where to take it from there."

Jané realizes just how much she likes her offer of loading his stuff up. It will be cathartic and give her much needed closure to pack up the remnants of her failed marriage and wedded hell in sealed boxes to be opened up and released somewhere else for Marilyn to deal with. Still, it makes her sad that Quon will no longer be a part of her life. He was the best thing in it for a long time, but neither does she feel as wrecked about it as she did. The good sex helped to exorcise some of the lingering 'what if's' and hard feelings that she would have suffered with if he had left her with just the bad memories of their marriage shredding before her eyes. It does not hurt either that he is already wondering who will take his place, or that Marilyn will lose Quon the same way she gained him; to another woman. Marilyn will probably become the nagging wife that wants to keep a close eye on him, constantly worrying about will he cheat on her like he cheated *with* her. He will hate that with a passion.

But I have to get his ass to leave first so he can be even more miserable than he is now. Maybe I was too lenient with the bastard and he went looking for a challenge somewhere else. I sincerely hope it was worth it for his sake.

Jané lifts a finger in the air and points it at the wall.

"Quon, the bathroom is *that* way."

His eyes start to rake contemptuously over her body.

"So you don't want to know where I'm moving to with another woman?" he inquires nastily, stunning her. He does not normally do nasty. Well, except for the last six months, but he was not *this* nasty even then.

Of course she wants to know where he is moving but she shakes her head, overcoming her curiosity. Wanting to know anything about him now is detrimental to her pledge to truly let him go.

"Why would I want to know, Quon, when I have my own places to go and people to see and do?" Jané has no problem with rubbing in her impending freedom in his face while he will gain a suspicious girlfriend.

He grimaces.

"What are you going to…" He stops to clear his throat and cross his arms over his chest.

"…*do* with them?"

If Jané did not know better, she would swear it physically hurt him to ask.

Good, her mind ejects the word acidly.

But, she shrugs and answers coolly, "Whatever I want. I have appetites I've never explored. I will now that I'm divorced."

Quon bends over until he is almost nose to nose with her.

"You're not divorced," he hisses.

She grins.

"Neither are you but that didn't stop you from banging Marilyn. Now someone gets to bang *me*."

He takes a step closer.

"If I find out you're fucking someone, Jané, I'll—"

She takes an intrusive step forward, cutting him and the tiny space left between them off.

"You'll what, Quon? Be upset? Oh I've been there. It's not so bad. Or maybe you'll try to hold on to me in a situation you have no control over? I've done that too and *that* hurts like hell. But I'll do your favor and tell you what you can do that hurts less. Suck it up and move on but I've got that T-shirt already so you'll have to get another one made."

She takes a step back.

"Now I'm over this. You should be too. Get your stuff and go home. You're not wanted here anymore."

He nods slowly and purses his lips, convincing Jané that he will do none of the things she advised.

"So you think I'm that easily replaced after all the screaming I made you do in our bedroom? I don't think so, Jané. You love me."

She shakes her head.

"Everyone is replaceable. *You* taught me that and you're not the only one with good sex. That is *my* bedroom. It's been that way for six months when I couldn't get you to make me scream at all. I did love you, Quon. Past tense like me when you met Marilyn so let me go, walk away, and stop worrying about who will occupy my bed and stop forgetting that you wanted a divorce."

"What if I don't want the divorce anymore?" he asks quietly.

"Too late. I gave you three times to select that option and you refused thinking the woman you wanted was somewhere else. And she is, waiting for you to divorce me, which you will do. Now get your stuff. And. Go. Home," she stresses.

"I. *Am*. Home," he counters stubbornly. Jané exhales wearily, not liking this new side to the man standing before her at all. She knows she has a hard decision to make if she wants to truly move on with her life.

"Okay, Quon, since I can't seem to get you to stay or go, *I'll* go. You stay."

He throws his head back and begins to laugh long and hard then returns his piercing glare to Jané's face.

"Where will you go?"

"I have options, Quon," she shrieks. "I've *always* had them. Hotels. My best friend's apartment. Or I could go home to my family in Georgia. I was never as big a burden as you thought I was, though

I was always the wife that could have given you more if you needed it. But you've found that more somewhere else already and can't change your mind *or* mine. What happened in that bedroom just now could have happened every night and maybe…" she pauses deliberately just to make the air pregnant with tension before finishing, "…if you're a good boy, it *might* happen again, but you can't make this separation or divorce difficult for me."

Jané is no idiot. It will be damn near impossible to find another man that can take her body to the places that Quon does. But, she does not want to screw all of Arizona to find Quon's replacement. So, she settles on bartering with sex to get him out of the house. He is becoming a petty, misogynistic toddler and she has never seen this side of him either. She starts to wonder does he have anymore sides. She hopes not while waiting for him to accept or decline her offer.

He exhales.

"Okay, Jané, I'll leave but I want to take you to dinner tomorrow… well tonight rather… and work on things between us. I know I made a royal mess of us. Maybe we can discuss what went wrong tonight and rebuild our relationship during the separation."

Jané wants to immediately scream, *'Royal mess! No, you made a colossal cluster fuck of things between us and you are the 'what' that went wrong!'*

But if she keeps participating in the conversation, it will only prolong Quon's stay. It is bad enough that he is suddenly stuck on hindsight mode, realizing that almost everything he needed was already waiting at home. In order to get him out of it, Jané decides she will have to appear to want the same thing he does.

"Sure, Quon? Where do you want to take me?" she asks casually with no intentions of going anywhere with him now or in the future, or building anything with the man that betrayed her without a second thought for her feelings.

A sudden smile breaks wide across his face. She does not prevent him from reaching for her hands to pull her closer. Then, images of their bodies linked together flood her head and make the usual fiery feelings for Quon rush her body. Her heart skips a beat as if to remind Jané of how much pain it is still in from the blow he delivered when he asked for a divorce. She doubts if she will be able to get him out of her heart anytime soon, if ever. But, the physical contact causing a conflict of interest between her heart and her body is one thing she can do something about. She extracts her hands from his and steps back.

"La Francine's on Thirty-Ninth will take us on short notice, Jané. I'll call you with the time," he mentions with a worried glance down at her hands dangling by her side. She nods, knowing Quon thinks that he is about to have his cake and eat it too.

But something will be missing from this party: me.

She is sure that Marilyn will be in attendance happily however.

"Can I have a kiss goodbye?" he inquires with a devilish grin.

Hell no!

Of course if she says that, he will want to know why.

So she says, "Ah…maybe later, I'm tired."

His smile widens to shameless arrogance.

"You should be. We turned each other out tonight."

"Listen, Quon. I'm really tired, but I have to turn on the alarm and make sure the door is locked after you leave sooo… if you could hurry up *please*. You wore me out and I'd really like to sleep now," she appeals.

He frowns then nods.

"Okay. I'll be quick but I still need to get my stuff out of the bathroom. Could you fix me some coffee to take with me? I have to go into the office early to prepare for a meeting."

She nods quickly. When Quon turns away to leave the closet, she releases a quiet sigh of relief then hurries downstairs, passing through the overly large living room into an enormous kitchen equipped with modern conveniences that would make any chef proud. She moves swiftly across the room to turn on the coffeepot that sits beside the glass-door fridge on a marble countertop against the farthest wall, and will brew Quon's favorite, hazelnut. Then, she swings around and treads quickly to the farmer's sink to haul a long silver flask from the glass cabinet above it. If she chose to, she could pretend this is a normal morning when she helps Quon off to work. But what good would that do her?

As soon as Marilyn turns up at work too, Quon will forget all about me again. No thanks.

Jané has had enough of living in denial. It only leads to more heartache when the truth surfaces.

She bends over the sink to rinse out the flask just as Quon walks up behind her, grabs her by the waist, and pulls her into his body like he used to do before Marilyn. Resentment for the other woman and Quon's desire for her begins to grow like a weed inside her. She turns the water off and steps sideways out of his reach before walking over to the coffeemaker. Fortunately for her, the ridiculously expensive machine makes quick work of filling the pot already a quarter full. She reaches for an empty pot on the countertop and switches them out so she can fill Quon's thermos. He usually goes right out the door afterwards. She hopes he will today, too.

She caps the cup and walks it over to Quon, who grabs it and traps her hand underneath his. She tries to pull away. His grip tightens, making her glare up at him.

"Jané," he whispers.

"Let me go, Quon," she murmurs back, hoping he hears the double meaning behind her words and heeds it.

After several very long seconds of looking probingly into her face, he releases her finally.

"I'm sorry, Jané. For everything." He sounds sincere but he sounded that way when he pledged to love her for better or worse, and look how well that worked out. Nor does his sincerity do shit for her heartache growing with his never-ending presence.

"It's okay, Quon. Just go." She almost adds, 'Marilyn is probably waiting,' but she knows that snide comment will only make him respond and stay longer.

He stares at her for what seems like forever before turning away to grab his things from an island in the middle of the kitchen housing a six aisle stove. A Gucci duffel bag that he usually uses for the gym waits with several plastic-coated suits still on the hanger. He slings the bag over his broad shoulder. The suits go over his forearm then he glances at her. She begins to pray silently that he will not say anything else. It is hard enough watching him prepare to walk out of the home they were happy in without him dragging it out. But it was even harder to see him leave every morning to go be with another woman while not knowing when or if he would return. Now, she stands rooted to the spot, doing her best to not see Quon at all.

He finally gets tired of her looking through him and swivels to leave by the garage access on the right side of the sink where his red Maserati is parked beside her blue Mercedes C-class. When the familiar sound of his driver side door opens and shuts, the soft echo through the room jars her out of the nothingness coating her mind. She moves swiftly to lock the door behind him, but does not know why she is in such a hurry. He has a key to every door in the house. She decides she needs to get the locks changed pronto then spins around and catches an unintentional glimpse of the time on the stainless steel microwave beside the matching coffee pot. It yells five thirty in the morning at her.

Damn, I have been up twenty-four hours.

And she is feeling every single minute that she has not slept since her marriage began its swift decline down the slippery slope of Quon's affair.

Well, at least it finally hit rock bottom.

Jané feels the irrepressible urge to sleep for a week. She is completely drained.

She creeps back into the bedroom and quickly falls asleep on her own pillow atop the covers. Dreams of Marilyn gloating in her face about stealing Quon away trouble her rest. What is even more disturbing is that Marilyn has no face, just a voice in the middle of pitch black blot above a lavender Prada pantsuit with no identity. Even while inside the nightmare, she understands the significance of the other woman's appearance. Marilyn had sucked up Jané's life like a black hole would, slowly swallowing everything Jané held near and dear until it left her with nothing and no identity. But she wants to know what Marilyn looks like, too. How could she not when the woman has her life?

An incessant ringing starts to permeate Jané's not so peaceful slumber. Marilyn, the black hole, keeps traipsing through her head. But, the ringing is worst. It is never-ending.

She finally comes to with a jerk and realizes it is the cordless house phone sitting on the side table that is demanding her attention. She reaches over, grabs it up before the shrilling stops, and checks the caller ID. Sullivan's Global is calling.

Quon. Damn.

She stabs the talk button and answers groggily, "Yeah."

"Sweetheart, wake up. It's two in the afternoon," he chirps into the mouthpiece, amused she is still in bed. She usually rises when he goes to work and stays up, waiting for him to return.

Looks like my schedule got blown to hell right along with my marriage.

Jané sits up.

"I'm woke, Quon."

"Good because dinner is at eight but I want to pick you up at six."

"Six! Why?" she shrieks, regretting the black hole she created for herself when she agreed to go out with him.

"I want to take you somewhere if you—" Quon stops talking. Something solid knocks the hell out of another object on his end.

Then someone starts yelling in the background.

"Quon!" A high-pitched yell pronounces his name without the 'n' on the end, giving it an exotic origin. Jané thinks maybe the speaker has one to.

"Who the hell are you talking to, Quon? Your wife? Or some other bitch you're fucking!"

Jané quickly settles on Marilyn being the hell raiser and heaves enough air out of her mouth to cause a tornado in China.

I hope Marilyn put herself at the top of the 'bitches fucking Quon' list and I'm not about to sit here and listen to this shit.

"Quon," Jané calls, irritated that his new life is already intruding in the middle of hers.

"Wait, Jané, let me handle this," he pleads.

"Marilyn! Get. Out. I'll call for you when I'm done on the phone," he adds in a harsh no nonsense tone. Jané lets her curiosity about their relationship get the best of her and keep her on the phone, waiting for Marilyn's reply in the elegant tone of a highly educated woman from somewhere other than North America.

"I'm not going anywhere until you tell me who you're taking out tonight," the other woman screeches. Jané sniggers into the line. Marilyn must have been eavesdropping, overheard more than she bargained for, and barged into Quon's office.

He does not get a chance to respond before Marilyn goes off again.

"I know it's that bitch wife of yours trying to hold on to you but you're mine now! You promised!"

Obviously, he makes lots of promises to lots of people but Jané is quickly becoming pissed off that the other woman is maligning her name like they share equal rights in his life, and she deserves no respect for being his wife.

Then, Quon's breath whooshes through the phone before he starts to speak quietly.

"Marilyn, if you call Jané one more bitch, you'll have a problem with me. Now leave before I *fire your ass*!" He loses his cool in the end and any chance to keep his office romance off the water cooler gossip list.

Marilyn fires back at the top of her voice, "Fire me! I'd like to see you try! Did you tell her we've been together for a year not six months? Did you tell her you brought me here from California two months after I moved there from Austria? How about that we met on your business trip and you poached me from another company?"

Jané listens avidly as Marilyn gives away details of their affair like soda escaping a shaken can while a brutal ache forms in her heart from learning about even more betrayal on her husband's part.

The shit has finally hit the fan and so has the truth. It always does after a breakup.

Now, Marilyn is fed up with waiting for Quon to be hers solely, forcing his hand when she does not have to.

Well damn, he didn't tell her that he asked for and got my agreement for a divorce, which means he really does not want one anymore. Too bad. Jané mocks to herself while the strong urge to screw Quon again, thoroughly, gathers momentum simply for the name-calling offense Marilyn has committed.

If she keeps it up, Jané will gladly go a step farther than cheating with her own husband to get back at her, and sue for half ownership of the company, make the judge force Quon to sell it, and put both their trifling asses out of work. But, Jané is already tired of hearing the slights to her person and more painful truth. It hurts her like she knew it would, and she has had it with pain being inflicted on her unjustifiably.

"Quon," she hisses.

"Jané, hold on, baby," he implores.

"*Baby!* Did you just call her baby with me standing—"

Marilyn's rant goes quiet abruptly along with the line which angers

Jané even more. She takes the phone from her ear and glares down at it.

This son of a bitch put me on hold. Not this time.

Jané is not about to sit on the shelf for another second after doing it for half a year. Quon will never get her to do it willingly again.

She hits the end button on the phone, tosses it onto the bed, and stands up to go in the bathroom. Two steps in, the phone rings again. Her trek stalls out as she ponders answering. Chances are damn good that Quon is calling back but other people call her from time to time, especially Simone who likes the end of the week the best for checking up on her.

Simone has been feeling some type of way for a while about Jané cutting herself off from everyone suddenly. She has mentioned often that she thinks Quon has been beating Jané, who always finds that hilarious before rushing Simone off the phone. She did not want to risk revealing that Quon has barely been home, even less touching her. Nevertheless, she has to start somewhere with informing everyone that her marriage is over. Who better to begin with than her best friend?

Who is violent! Shit, Simone will threaten to separate Quon from his man parts and try to if she sees him. But he brought that shit on himself.

Jané has no qualms about Quon being able to defend himself and reaches for the phone. She laughs out loud when the ID divulges that it is indeed Simone calling, and cannot answer the phone fast enough.

"Hey, girl." She drops back onto the bed.

"Hey, yourself stranger. What's popping?" Simone asks cheerfully.

Jané sighs.

"Everything is popping…*dropping…changing.*"

"Things finally came to a head, huh?" Simone's chipper tone simmers down.

"Yep. I'll be divorced in a little while."

Simone sucks up all the air between Arizona and Atlanta and hisses, "What the fuck has been going on in that house?"

"Nothing until last night. I confronted Quon about his late nights and early mornings. He asked for a divorce. Now I need life," she replies dryly.

"Jané, you're making this seem like you brought the wrong spaghetti sauce and you need to go back to the store."

"Hmmm…that about sums it up," she counters.

Simone starts to giggle.

"No you need to get out that damn house. Meet me after work today. I need to get some things done to myself."

Jané becomes curious, and glad Simone is taking this so well.

"What things?"

"The works, wax, trim, facial. You know the things we do for men."

Jané knows she could do with all of that herself, but *for* herself.

"Okay, what time?" The line gets eerily quiet. "Simone!"

"I'm here. Just shocked you're willing to come out and spend some time with your best friend now."

Jané starts to feel guilty for alienating everyone.

"Simone, I was hiding the troubles in my marriage from everyone, hoping it would get better, and I wouldn't have to tell anyone about them. I haven't talked to my family in Atlanta at all but I'm good now, ready to move on."

"*That* fast, Jané?" she asks disbelievingly. "After only *hours* of being single?"

Jané knows she owes Simone an explanation for dropping their friendship like a hot potato with no notice.

"I've been single for six months," she admits quietly. "I just couldn't accept things were really over in my marriage until last night. I've cried so much I could have flooded the Pacific Ocean. Quon only came home to sleep. Other than that we were roommates." Then the line beeps in Jané's ear.

"Hold on, Simone."

She looks at the screen reading Sullivan Global.

Quon again. Too bad.

She puts the phone back to her ear.

"So anyway, Simone, what time is you going for the works and where?" She did not feel the need to mention her future ex is calling. After wishing for months that he would, she did not feel any obligation to acknowledge him either, or his dinner invitation that he is probably calling about. Jané has not cooked in two months because she had no one to eat with. She sure as hell was not going to change that now, and realizes that she had already taken a tiny step towards accepting that Quon was becoming her husband on paper only without even noticing it. She begins to wonder how many more steps had she taken unconsciously.

"I have a five thirty at Sensual Salon." Simone says suddenly. "They're very good for a lot less money than the uptown spas charge. You know the ones you would go to, Jané, if you weren't so beautiful already," she jests.

"Simone, I haven't been or felt beautiful in months."

"That's acceptable when someone you love more than yourself turns away from you. The first thing we do is ask what is wrong with me. But we are *not* responsible for someone else's decisions though we suffer like hell because of them," Simone stresses angrily, not needing to get upset while at work. There will be enough time at the spa for that when Jané tells her the dirty details of Quon's affair.

"Simone, do I need to call and make an appointment or do they take walk-ins?" Jané asks for purposes of changing the subject.

Simone breathes heavily into phone.

"Don't worry about it. I'll call and make sure they can take a double visit or change the time so we can go together or somewhere else if they can't. Nothing will interfere with our girl time today. I've missed you too much for that, Jané."

Jané's eyes begin to burn as overwhelming love for her surrogate sister engulfs her.

"I've missed you too, Simone, and promise to explain why I was MIA. Maybe you'll understand. Maybe you won't. But I love you for not giving up on me."

Simone giggles.

"Believe me, Jané, I thought about it but couldn't do it without knowing if you were okay first. And if I see Quon, I swear—"

"Simone!" Jané cuts her off. She does not want her getting anymore worked up than she already is. "He is not worth the emotional overload or jail time. I thought he was but—" The line beeps again, Sullivan Global again.

Jané keeps talking.

"But he isn't and he has troubles of his own brewing now." Then she giggles, remembering Marilyn's performance as a nagging girlfriend already promising to be a showstopper. But Quon's reputation in the good ole boy's world of scandalous office romances will not be harmed although Marilyn's will.

You'd think she is smart enough to know that women seldom get away with the same shit men do. I guess she isn't and she'll deserve everything she loses for being stupid.

"What's funny, Jané?" Simone asks suspiciously.

"I'll tell you everything at the spa or bar or wherever we end up," she chirps back.

"That you will, my dear. Now let me hit you back when I've taken care of your appointment at the spa. I'm killing my minutes with this expensive ass cell company I use and will text you the time and *or* place." Simone's income is that of a struggling artist though she is a secretary for a wealthy snob that does not recognize the efforts of any woman in his employ, and has Simone on ten by her first break every day. But, she knows how to make do with the peanuts she earns and treats herself every chance she gets just to deal with a stressful workplace. If smoking was allowed at her desk, Simone would happily become a chain smoker.

"Okay, Simone. I can't wait to see you, girl, and I promise to never let another man come between us."

"You better not either. I've been bored out of my fucking mind without you. Nobody can stand to be around my ass that long," she quips except there is a lot of truth to her words. Simone is foul mouthed and short tempered.

"Stop threatening to kick everybody's ass and maybe more than me could handle you at your worst."

Simone gasps.

"I don't threaten! I make damn promises! If I wasn't so good at my job, I probably wouldn't have it *or* get another one." Then she laughs. "I'm out, Jané. Be looking for my message and don't make me come over there to get you."

Jané snorts.

"Bye, Simone."

Simone snickers and hangs up. Jané tosses the phone in the rumpled folds of the bed covers and gets up to retrieve the first pair of jeans, tennis shoes, and white V-neck tee that she sees. This time, she makes it successfully into the bathroom where she executes a quick morning routine and throws her hair in a sleek ponytail at the back of her head. Unfamiliar hunger pangs drive her into the kitchen where she fixes toast and orange juice to consume while leaning against the sink.

She lets her eyes roam the room, remembering happier moments that withstood the test of time though her marriage did not. Moments like when she and Quon first moved in and christened this room four years ago. Just yesterday, no one would have been able to convince her that he would one day betray her and demand she let him go. That was not supposed to happen to them. But it did and she had to find new moments to crystallize in her mind and let the old ones become irrelevant. Quon had.

She shakes her head, clearing away the images of the past. She refuses to be the only one haunted by them, and promises to never let them inside her head again. They do not belong there anymore, or in her heart.

I will harden it and never let another man in there either. I am better off alone.

Chapter Four

After finishing her meager breakfast, she goes back upstairs to make a call to the first moving company she finds in the phone book stashed in the night table.

"Daniel's," a deep voice answers and triggers Jané's nosiness. She begins to wonder how many women has it lulled to sleep, or into danger they would happily risk just to be near whoever owns the voice. When it asks for her info then gives an estimated time for the moving men's arrival, she says thank you, hangs up, forgets about it, and starts to strip the bed.

She focuses solely on replacing the linens with ones fresh out of the laundry and the process of erasing any sign of her and Quon together. That includes dropping the picture beside the bed of their smiling faces on their wedding day encased in beveled silver into the top drawer of her nightstand. Then, she grabs her purse and keys from it and rides to the nearest store with Lyfe Jennings' emotionally packed "Boomerang" hit playing loudly from her speakers for company. She buys a bundle of boxes and packing material while planning to scour the house for every trace of Quon that she cannot bear to look at when she gets back.

For a moment, she considers creating a scene straight out of *Waiting to Exhale* with Quon's precious possessions, but he no longer deserves that big of a performance or magnitude of emotions from her. Besides, burning anything even outside the city limits of Tucson is a crime, and Jané thinks she is being punished enough.

Her sense of betrayal will have to settle for shipping his belongings to the next woman that he will make suffer.

Marilyn will be more than happy to receive them, she thinks dryly.

As soon as Jané unlocks the front door, the same ringing that woke her up greets her entry. She grabs the nearest phone off its base hidden in one of many alcoves of an enormous oak entertainment center. It almost covers a whole wall in the living room, and Sullivan's Global is calling *again*.

Jané does not want to talk to anyone that works there. She mutes the ringer on the phone, tosses it back in the same dark pocket it came from along with her purse, and goes right back out the door to her car. She opens the trunk concealing the horde of boxes she is not sure how to get out then inside the house because she is not sure how the store's bagboy got them in. She hopes that she will not need many, which gives her the idea to just grab one at a time, and begins sawing through the twine holding them together with her car key. When it finally pops, she grabs the top container, slams her trunk closed, and does an awkward dance all the way back to the front door with the bulky box almost taller than her five-feet-four stature. When she enters the living room, a song is playing barely audible upstairs.

Jané knows for a fact that the CD player stopped spinning hours ago.

"So what the hell is that noise and where is it coming from?" she asks no one in particular, and damn sure she did not want to be the one to go looking for the answer. But somebody has to and she is it.

She drops the box in the floor and scales the stairs warily until the song's lyrics get clearer and recognizable, Phyllisia's "I Love You". It is her ringtone for Quon on a cell phone she has not thought about or used in the last month, but keeps it charged out of habit. She did not need it because she rarely left the house and did not stay away from it too long in case Quon called, hopefully to pick up where he left off in their marriage when she least expected it. Jané wanted to be available when he did.

She missed the times when he would drive home from work to have lunch with her or just have her. She realizes the lunch dates had started to taper off before the old Quon disappeared, and her habit of grabbing the cell phone when she went out dissipated with his visits home.

Thanks to Quon's sorry ass, I'll have to relearn a whole bunch of simple shit that single women do all the time, like remembering this damn cell phone and taking that stinking trashcan to the curb on garbage day. Fuck. You. Quon.

Jané snatches open the same drawer with the snapshot of her wedding day face down in it then tunnels her finger under the frame to drag out the cell, no longer ringing but releasing single beeps, alerting her to a voicemail. Her screen boasts several missed calls and a message from Sullivan's Global, making her shake her head despairingly. Quon is annoying the hell out of her with his persistence. She starts to wonder is he trying to make up for all the times he has not called, and wishes he would stop if he is.

She presses one on the keypad to listen to the voicemail.

Quon's troubled voice comes through loud and clear though he should not remember she has the mobile either.

"Jané, baby, I'm sorry I put you on hold for so long. I had to have Marilyn's crazy ass escorted from the building. She's no longer a problem for us, sweetheart…*shit*…and I'm sorry I didn't realize what I had until it was gone. Anyway I know you probably want nothing to do with me but I still…*beep*." Time had run out on Quon, and Jané feels like it is a sign to let the same happen for their communication. Not to indulge in tit for tat, but because he is a no good bastard who broke her heart and it is entirely possible he will do it again if she takes him back. She is not about to sign up for that what if nor able to handle another moment in that world. She is out of it and staying that way.

Quon will just have to make up with Marilyn's crazy ass.

Jané is not amazed they have already fallen apart. She knew it was coming and they should have too.

They would have if they had bothered to look past each other to the havoc their affair was wreaking on the world around them, mine!

Blind rage begins to swim through her.

Greedy, selfish ass people that took no account of what they would lose for a goddamn fling squatting on a foundation that it did not belong on.

That foundation is Jané's life, and she and it both are done with bearing the consequences of Quon's and Marilyn's actions.

She slips the phone in her back pocket and takes the stairs at a fast clip, more than ready to pack Quon's life in boxes and get them out of hers. A tiny lighting rod skims up her backside, catching her off guard. She arches forward to escape the mysterious sensation and glances back simultaneously, nearly throwing her spine out of place by trying to see what is clamoring for her attention or electrocuting her with very low wattage. Only then does she realize it is her phone vibrating against her butt. She straightens up and starts to laugh at her own silliness while retrieving the phone.

I can't even remember how normal things in life feel.

Jané wishes she knew how long it is going to take before she does.

She activates the screen, finding a text waiting, and taps the icon. Simone is confirming their dual session at Sensual's for five thirty. Jané hopes maybe they can fit in a night out. It is not like she has a reason to spend them around the house anymore and she sure as hell does not want to follow her usual routine of being here alone. Her phone starts to vibrate in her hand before a sudden, melodic 'I love you' smashes the silence in the room. She cringes when Sullivan's Global appears across the screen again.

"Come on, Quon! Catch a damn hint already," she yells before ignoring the call, turns off the vibration then ringer, and drops the phone back in her pocket. Next, she snatches the box off the floor and begins packing Quon's things. The boxes quickly grow out of control in the living room and bedroom. Anything that holds a memory of their time together went in them. She is no longer hosting a packing party of one but an outright purge. Decorations brought on shared trips to the store went in. Knick knacks he breathed on did, too. Even pictures on the wall had to go.

Quon is into acquiring art big time from well-known painters to those working street side to earn a buck. She does him a favor of bubble wrapping them before leaning each one carefully against boxes already sealed and waiting to be shipped. When her stomach begins to feel hollow from hunger, a knock at the door delays her march into the kitchen. She checks the glistening gold clock on the living room wall, the only thing still hanging and pointing to four o'clock on the dot. The hours have flown by. The moving company has arrived. The time for Quon to become a permanent fixture in her past is here.

Jané trudges to the door while dodging cardboard obstacles and opens it.

A blond man with masses of muscles on a frame an inch or less taller than and twice as wide as Quon stands in her doorway, blocking out the daylight.

"We're from Daniel's Moving Company. Are you Mrs. Sullivan?"

She manages to nod while trying not to stare rudely, instantly pins the voice on the phone to him, and barely stops herself from giving him full god status. Her manner insists that she opens the door wider, figures that he will need the space to get inside with his size, and steps to the side.

He steps over the threshold while scanning her home warily. Two short and slim brunette men that look like they should be in college follow him in, leaving one tall black man with well-maintained dreads hanging to his sculptured ass framed in khakis on the porch. A green polo shirt coats his back that is turned while he speaks into his phone belligerently. She frowns at the mover who obviously does not realize that she has opened the door or how much she needs him to haul Quon's belongings out of here.

"Ms. Sullivan, if you could direct us to the room we'll be clearing of boxes, we can get them out of your way faster," blond god suggests. Jané spins on her heels and begins leading the way upstairs, immediately feeling like the man's eyes is digging into her back. She quickly becomes self-conscious. She has not taken the best care of herself lately, and almost glad that she has not. She is not looking for a replacement for Quon that her best would probably bring. So why even be concerned about their view of her casual appearance?

She does not know why but she is, and her visit to the spa with Simone cannot come fast enough.

While guiding the men into her bedroom, Jané comprehends she needs to reset her self-respect and confidence in the image the mirror presents again. Quon has done more damage to her psyche than she realized.

"Mrs. Sullivan," the deep voice from the phone, calls to her. She spins to face the owner in gorgeously tanned flesh who is staring at her, apparently perplexed by her sudden silence that must have gone on for much longer than acceptable.

"Ah…sorry. This is the only other room with boxes. I'll leave you to your job." Then, she walks out without excusing herself before the man can say something else about the oddness of her behavior, or see more of it.

She slips down the stairs and out the opened front door then steps onto a tiny cobbled sidewalk circling the house to the back deck. But, she stops under her bedroom window before she gets there. If she could, she would have the back of the house hauled off, too. That is where she sat most nights waiting for Quon. She has been alone for so long, being in the company of others, especially men, is unsettling. Normally, she would have said something witty to cover her moodiness but her frame of mind is still in self-preservation mode. Keeping Quon's secret has made her guarded, hoping the world does not see right through her to the layer of failure just beneath her skin. His betrayal has changed her, tainted her, and made her a stranger to her own self.

Jané suspects she has lost her self-worth and identity by allowing Quon to treat her badly for too long, a lot longer than she thought. According to Marilyn, he has been living a double life for twice as long.

How could I not see it?

She stands completely frozen in time, allowing her mind to flip through moments in her marriage that did not seem odd at the time. She instinctively knows that is where she will find her answer and the warning signs that she brushed off stupidly. When nothing unusual jumps out at her, she gets angry with herself for not staying in college to hone her detective skills and letting Quon's life and schedule absorb hers. His work hours did not change suddenly so she could see the change in him immediately. Then, Jané feels the urge to smack herself upside the head hard but resists.

You're an idiot, Jané. His hours may have changed slowly but they changed and your dumb ass still missed it.

Jané suddenly remembers Quon stopped coming home for lunch, around the same time his appetite for sex decreased from seven or six times a week to four and three then one until nothing a *year* ago. At the time, she chalked it up to the fire dying between them as it does in all relationships. So, she focused on making him see her again, not if he was seeing someone else.

The signs were right there. All I had to do was look. How could I be so stupid and not look?

Jané does not get a chance to answer her own question because a presence emerges at her backside.

"Mrs. Sullivan," the same voice that called to her upstairs calls again before she can turn around.

"Yes," she answers while spinning on her heels. The man smiles down at her, her head only reaching his chin. She feels tiny compared to his size and the massive sinew draping his upper torso.

She cannot help but stare at his chest. It seems to be made especially for a woman to plant both hands on it and lean into when the world becomes too much to stand alone in, like now. She feels an overwhelming desire to do it, balls her hands beside her hips instead.

"You okay?" he asks concerned, his smile disappearing and forehead wrinkling.

Not really.

But she is not going to tell him that, so she nods her head.

"I'm fine. What can I do for you?"

He frowns.

"You sure? You seemed a million miles away again."

"I was," she admits. "Life is…*different* for me now. I'm trying to figure out when it changed and where I fit."

He nods as his brow smoothes out.

"You're getting divorced, aren't you?"

Her mouth falls open in surprise.

"How did you…damn. Am I that obvious?" she whispers, freaked out of her mind that he can read her so easily. She never told him he would be moving only her husband's thing and cannot handle everybody knowing all at once that she is no longer Mrs. Sullivan. She does not know who the hell she is now or want anyone to figure it out before she does, and wanted to ease into her new status of becoming Jané Davidson again. Now, she wonders if **divorcée** is written across her damn forehead.

The man grins.

"You're not obvious. I just recognize the signs because I've been there."

"What signs?" she asks urgently, needing to know so she can get rid of them.

"The spacing out to wonder in peace about how did you not see the divorce coming. You're packing only half of the house, and not all that comfortable in our presence which means you decided to lay off of men for a while, if not for life."

Damn, he's good.

Jané nods her confirmation to all the above, seeing no point in denying any of it to someone who has already been down this road and knows when someone else is traveling it. She finds common ground with the man and wonders what else he is good at.

Do not go there, Jané. You just got out of a bad relationship.

But, she has to confess that it was not all bad. The beginning was a fairytale and what she needed right after her family's death. Her throat tightens with emotions as usual when she thinks of her parents gone too soon. She clears them away with a deep swallow and stops staring at the man's chest to stare into his ocean blue eyes under thick gold lashes.

"Yeah, I thought he was cheating for the last six months but it was really a year. He asked for a divorce last night. I decided to go quietly…or rather pack his things that way." Then, she recalls the other things that Quon took with him this morning, not his bag but the memories of their ex sex. She begins to grin.

He could not have left those images behind if he tried.

Blond god smirks and cocks his head. The subtle expression gives him a curious little boy air, and appeals way too much to Jané for her comfort.

"What did you do, Mrs. Sullivan? And yeah that smile is *very* obvious." Next, he laughs, making her grin harder and want to tell him about her tiny revenge that sparked a great divide between Quon and his mistress.

"I gave him a few memories to take with him to his new home. Now he doesn't want to go there, but to dinner with me and I won't answer his calls," she gloats unashamedly.

He chuckles quietly while probing Jané's face.

"You screwed him six ways from Sunday, didn't you?" he asks straightforward. She nods quickly and releases a devious smile to play on her lips while appreciating his bluntness. She has had enough of lies and deceit for two lifetimes.

He laughs even louder and absorbs her attention again.

"That's why your back pocket keeps lighting up, huh? It's your husband hoping you're not screwing another man or at least with their head like you did his."

Jané folds her arms across her chest as her thoughts take off.

Supposed I did screw someone else? Would I feel better about my marriage and everything as I know it ending? Probably not.

She figures she will have to work through her heartbreak the same way Quon introduced her to it, slowly.

The man standing before her narrows his eyes to mere slits.

"What's going on in that gorgeous head of yours?" he asks warily.

She scoffs.

"There's nothing gorgeous about me. Your eyes must be bad, Mr....ah." Only then does she realize that she has divulged her troubles and a few secrets to a complete stranger, and it was too easy to do. Good thing she will never see him again and he does not know the details of what else she allowed Quon to do to her. She is not sure how he will look at her after that conversation.

The man stretches his huge hand out to her with a lopsided smile, making one eye crinkle around the corner adorably.

"I'm Blazier Freeman. My friends call me Blaze."

She takes his hand. Tiny tingles race across her palm, and she feels why they call him Blaze. Her insides start to overheat from the flesh-to-flesh contact. She decides to stick with Blazier. Familiarity at this point will not breed contempt on her end, but more lust that she does not want while she is still married.

"I'm Jané," she whispers then lets his hand go. She did not want to, which is why she did. She knows attraction when she feels it, which is so bad for her vows. She wants to believe there is some loyalty still left in her world when it comes to the opposite sex, even if it only comes from her.

Blazier knits his hands together in front of his crotch, drawing her eyes to the bulge there. He widens his stance like he is making room for an unwanted erection.

I hope that it is an erection because if he is that huge while soft...

Jané refuses to finish the thought but cannot do a damn thing about her core tightening.

So not good.

"So, Jané, what are you doing to get back on your feet?" he asks suddenly.

She scoffs again.

"I never had my feet *under* me. I met my husband in college and let him convince me to quit a year before I graduated with promises that he will take care of and love me forever. We moved here from Georgia so he could start his business here where he has no competition. But there is plenty for me, obviously. He's done very well for himself."

"Now what are you going to do for *yourself*? I know your self-esteem is low. So were mine and everyone else's that has been screwed over by the ones they love. We all go through the 'what did we lack' stage, and we did lack something, a good sense of judgment about the people we loved. Now love yourself," he insists sternly, inciting Jané to wonder what idiot made the bad decision to let this man go and when was the last time that she did anything for herself without Quon in mind. She cannot remember but today's spa visit will be a good start. She smiles, not seeing anything wrong with pleasing herself and only herself for the first time since she got married.

"I'm going on a date with my best friend after you guys remove my future ex from my life," she confesses easily.

Blazier frowns.

"You know he's not going to go away as easy as he did when he was cheating?"

Her smile turns upside down instantly. She has never dealt with a cheater before now and does not know the rules for this sort of thing.

"Why not?" she shrieks. "It was easy for him to step out on me! It was easy for him to ask for a divorce! It was easy for him to ignore my existence and feelings!" Her anger rises with each point she ticks off verbally. Why Quon would make her life any more difficult than he already has, she has not the faintest idea.

Blazier stands up straight and spears her with a piercing glance, warning her that more truth she may not want to hear is incoming.

"Because you were still a part of his life taking care of the things the other woman didn't when he made those mistakes, Jané. Her purpose is to do all the things you couldn't, or wouldn't, or didn't even know you needed to do. He'll realize if he hasn't already, that all the things he'll lose won't be worth the divorce. Just the thought of you doing everything for someone else that you did for him will make him cling to you. He'll start to hate the changes he brought on himself," he warns.

"That's not fair," she yells. "I didn't ask him to go looking for what he needed in another woman and he never said he was lacking at home!" Her emotions quickly rage out of control from just thinking about Quon's selfish choices that ruined her life.

"It could be he wasn't looking for anything but a new challenge." Blazier says suddenly, cutting into her emotional implosion. "Men are wired to spread their seed around while hoping no lasting evidence will connect him to his actions."

She loses it.

"Well, he asked for a way out, Blazier! I gave it to him because if he can hurt me like that, he didn't deserve anything I was or wasn't doing for him!" She is becoming heartbroken all over again. It is like Quon is standing before her and asking for a divorce all over again.

"What did I do that was so bad he needed to love someone else?" she asks in a whisper overloaded with pain for her loss. If Quon was dead, she could not be hurt more. Only then does she realize that by asking that question, she is giving herself all the blame for the breakdown of her marriage.

I may not be blameless either because I ignored the warnings of him moving away in his heart, but I sure as hell don't deserve the bulk of the blame.

Jané would have done anything to keep her husband, maybe everything.

But if my complete submission and willingness to please him couldn't keep him loving me, nothing else I did would have either.

Jané does not think the man she married is really the one she loves, not if he can treat her and Marilyn, who is now also regulated to the edges of Quon's life, like they are expendable.

However, she does question if she gave Quon all the qualities she thought he already possessed, and becomes extremely unhappy about him suddenly wanting to rekindle the fire in their marriage after he finds a freaky side to his wife.

How long before he gets bored with that and seeks out new territory to conquer again?

Jané decides she does not want to find out. There are too many Marilyn's in the world willing to take her place. Quon is a good catch, a cheating, lying, traitorous one, but the Marilyn's will still bite any bait he throws out.

Blazier takes a tiny step toward Jané like he is afraid he will spook her. When she focuses on his blurry profile, she contemplates why he is fuzzy.

Oh damn. I'm crying.

She covers her face with her hands, and whispers into her palms, "I'm sorry, Blazier." She is utterly embarrassed that she cracked up then broke down in front of him, and takes huge gulps of her own carbon dioxide trapped in her hands, hoping to calm the tirade still stewing inside. When she thinks she has control of her emotions, she removes her fingers to swipe at the damnable tears.

"It's okay, Jané," he says softly. "You have to feel it to get through it then past it. If you push the pain back now, it will manifest in another area of your life later until you acknowledge it, and it won't go away overnight. What you went through didn't happen overnight. Take your time and get to know the new you because you have been changed forever. But it doesn't have to be a bad thing."

She stares at him as his words sink in, making her feel even worse that the moving man pities her. He did not know her from a lick of furniture but still trying to comfort her all the same as if they are friends.

"Why are you telling me all of this? You don't know me," she murmurs.

His lopsided smile returns.

"Because I wish someone had told me being divorced isn't the end of the world or mine. I went down a lot of bad roads after my wife left me. Some I wasn't even trying to but I wouldn't acknowledge my pain and it *pushed* me down them. At some point, she told me that I was the good thing in her life she didn't appreciate. She also told me that I needed to stop hurting myself for her mistakes and following in her footsteps, destroying everything around me."

Jané becomes curious about the outcome of his story, wanting to know how he became the man he is today after that kind of pain. She stubbornly ignores that he is a stranger with a right to keep the things that he did not want to tell her to himself. She is intrigued, and about to be rude.

"Well what happened next? I'm sorry to ask how you survived this and can still be the good man that you seem to be, but my world is upside down and I'm not sure if it will ever be right again. Though I want it to be."

"I took my ex's advice and got my shit together," he says simply.

"So you two didn't get back together?" she asks disbelievingly. If his ex really let him go, then she really is an idiot.

"Nope, but not because she didn't offer. I no longer trusted her. You can't be with someone you can't trust even if you love them. You'll worry more about the next hit of pain they'll cause you than loving them." In other words, the relationship wouldn't have lasted no matter what they did differently in it, and that is exactly how Jané feels about Quon. She has worried about his hurtful ass enough.

She finally nods after getting her answer.

Blazier releases a grin at full wattage then asks, "Feel better?" Oddly, she does but does not know if his smile did the trick or talking about a shared tragedy with someone that understands. She nods again simply, feeling a little less burdened by her circumstances and not so alone in them anymore.

"That's what I wanted. Now, can I give you some free advice?"

Jané cocks an eyebrow skeptically. She thought giving her free advice is what he was already doing. But she is still fascinated with the strange man that has made her world a little less dark in so short a time. He has a way of speaking without sounding self-righteous to her about the afterlife of a dead marriage that makes her listen. She finds it weird she likes that he has been in her shoes, even though she would not wish them on anyone else's feet, except Marilyn's.

That bitch wanted them. She can have them.

Jané finally nods again for him to continue.

"Get out of the house often or you'll sit here, dissect your divorce, analyze, and come up with the wrong reasons why your life is beginning again *not* ending. You have to live with your husband's decisions but they don't have to define you."

Then, someone walks around the side of the house in Jané's peripheral, and asks, "Can I ask why you two are discussing *my* decisions without me?"

Oh God, Quon has come home and caught me talking to another man about him. What the hell do I do now?

Chapter Five

Jané stiffens, remembers she is single, and rethinks her thoughts hurriedly while Quon comes to a standstill only a few feet away to glare at them both.

Quon has come here and heard me talking to another man about him. I have nothing to feel guilty about.

Now, she just needs to convince herself to embody that mode of thinking. Being married and worried about how her husband feelings were her only way of life, and she would get use to that, even if it kills her.

She turns sideways to face him.

"Hello, Quon. This is Blazier. He's with the moving company that will bring your stuff to your office. Since you're here for once, *you* can tell them where Marilyn lives and save them a trip," she says casually like nothing is off.

It isn't, she insists silently. She can talk to anyone about anything at anytime when she gets ready now.

"Oh, and Blazier was giving me advice about life after divorce," she explains for cruel purposes. She wants to remind Quon where they both stand now, apart.

He scowls at her.

"Can I talk to you privately for a minute, Jané?"

She exhales, frustrated that she failed to avoid this conversation, and positive it involves them not being divorced yet, as if she did not already know that.

Blazier reaches over and taps her lightly on the elbow. Tiny nips of electricity zip up her arm, leaving a trail of goose bumps in their wake. Jané did not think anyone else's touch could cause her body to react at the smallest touch like Quon's does, and it is distressing and too soon.

"I'll go, Jané, but you have some opened boxes in the bedroom I wanted to ask about. But I'll wait for you to come back inside," Blazier says quietly then walks off.

"Wait," she says quickly, not really wanting to be alone with Quon. Blazier stops and glances back. "Close the boxes and I will check behind you after you've moved them all to make sure you didn't leave anything." He nods then walks toward Quon, who is standing on the sidewalk and does not look like he is going to move. Blazier steps into the grass, goes around Quon. Then, he steps back onto the sidewalk.

Quon's glare gets harsher as if he wanted Blazier to try him for the carefully placed stones Jané laid herself. When Blazier does not, Quon bristles and clenches his fists at his side like he wants to hit someone, or say something to them. He glances back and hurls over his shoulder, "She's married you know."

Blazier keeps walking. Jané knows an altercation on the job could cost him his and she silently applauds him for not risking it to argue with Quon. She watches him turn the corner of the house without responding, knowing instantly who the better man is; the one that had been broken and restarted life again.

She turns her gaze to Quon. She still has a date to keep and wants this damn conversation over with since she cannot avoid it.

"What is it, Quon?"

"You know he just wants to sleep with you right?"

A volcano of snickers erupts in her chest. She finds it funny that he is upset because someone might actually want what he left behind.

"What's it to you? Is it so bad that someone might take your leftovers?" she asks condescendingly. "And for your information, I don't think that someone is Blazier."

Quon's face lessens in intensity.

"You're not my leftovers, Jané, and I was stupid to ask for a—" She swipes her hand through the air before he can even go there.

"Stop, Quon. I don't have time for this and neither do you. We both have somewhere to be."

He steps forward and drops both hands on her shoulders. The flesh under his touch tingles too, but this reaction is familiar to her and not so disturbing. Or maybe it should be.

She almost groans aloud when she has to accept that her cheating ass husband is still in her heart *and* her system. Right now, both are remembering how he feels in her body, too heavenly to let go of the memories apparently.

So not fucking good.

"Jané," he whispers, "We can get through this."

She smiles weakly then steps back until his hands fall away. She becomes a little sad that he is counting the cost of losing their marriage too late, but he has a long way to go before he reached the end of the long lists of benefits that he had as her husband.

"We *will* get through this, Quon. I promise."

He grins from ear to ear.

"Should I tell them to move my stuff back inside?"

Jané laughs in his face. She hates to admit that she is actually enjoying the hopeful but pointless gleam in his eyes. However, it is nice to see it in his and not the mirror for once.

"Not a chance. We will get through this like we went into it, *apart*. You will get out as planned. You will get the divorce as planned. You will get on with your life as…say it with me…*planned*. These are your plans, remember?"

He grimaces as the hopeful look in his eyes fades.

"But, Jané, I thought we were working on us. I got rid of Marilyn for you," he appeals softly. She shakes her head, regretful that he is seeing things how he wants to and making this split harder than it has to be. It seems that no matter what she says he only hears what he wants to, too.

"Quon, look closely at my mouth then listen to what comes out of it. We. Are. Done. There is no fixing this. We can become friends, maybe even lovers, but our time being married is up." She speculates how many times she will have to say this to him before it becomes real to him. She hopes not too many. She still had to get the moving men on their way.

He starts to shake his head.

"Jané, I'm sorry," he whispers. She also wonders how many times he will say that.

"Quon, I get it. You. Are. Sorry. But it doesn't undo any of the pain you caused."

He sighs.

"I know—"

"Then go to Marilyn and fix what you broke with her *please*."

Anger envelops his face, making his mouth tight.

"That bitch ruined everything," he utters suddenly, and pushes Jané past her breaking point again.

"*She* didn't ruin us. *You* did. This was your home. I was your wife. It was your marriage going down the tubes. All your responsibility. Now Marilyn is all you have left. *Own it,*" she finishes in a yell.

"I do, Jané, now let me fix it. Don't let someone else like Blazier, where the hell did his mama come up with that name, come between us."

"Oh, you think only people with common names like Marilyn should come between us? You forget. There *is* no between us anymore." That fact hits home again for Jané. Her anger spills over and drives her closer to Quon to point a finger in his face.

"You hadn't even fully left me for Marilyn yet and you've already screwed somebody else, *me*. I became the other woman last night, Quon, and you didn't give her a second thought after you threw everything away for her. You can't fix that. It's done."

His forehead wrinkles then he yells, "Other woman? Jané, you're my wife! What are you talking about?"

"I haven't been your wife for a year. I was your roommate, maid, cook, number one fan, and now the other woman. She had your time, body, heart, and your mind. Now take your material possessions and be hers completely."

Jané's chest heaves from her rant, unable to believe he is having this much trouble letting her go. He really is regretting his affair, or conveniently forgetting that he had one. Both are bad for her and Marilyn.

"Jesus, Jané, give me a chance to make this right," he pleads at the top of his voice.

She shakes her head as if that movement will convey what her words cannot.

"You can't now. I gave you six months for that. Now you're doing the same thing you did to me to someone else. No one means anything to you. I don't deserve that. You can't have me back so please for God's sake let this go."

While Jané ponders how she became the one doing the begging again, Quon's hands reach up and capture her shoulders again. His fingertips dig into them uncomfortably. She does not like his touch right now even if it does not hurt. So, she squirms under his hold but it does not help in liberating her.

"Jané, please, *don't* do this to me."

She stops fidgeting to peer up at him.

"Why not, Quon? You did it to me. Now let me go. You're almost hurting me."

"Mrs. and Mr. Sullivan, is everything okay?" Blazier asks, suddenly behind Quon.

Quon glances back and shouts, "Don't you see me talking to my wife?"

Blazier walks closer until he stands beside them. He peers down at Jané.

"Are you okay?" he asks coolly like he is not concerned about Quon's behavior, but Jané sure as hell is. She has never known him to yell at anyone, recognizes him only as a lover, not a screamer.

She reaches up and lifts his hands off her shoulders, knowing that he let her. Then, she steps several paces back. He raises an accusing thumb in the air and gifts Jané with a black glare.

"Is *he* your new man now and the reason you don't want me back? Have you been sleeping with him?" he asks in a shout that makes Jané flinch with each accusation that he flings at her. She slips down a steep incline of shock that he could think she would do any of the hurtful things he did to her.

"Quon," she whispers. "I just met him thirty minutes ago. The only cheat out here is you. You need to leave."

"This is still my home. I'm not going anywhere. No other man will ever take what's mine," he hisses. Jané looks at him peculiarly. She does not know this Quon; possessive, angry, and bordering on violent. But, she does know someone has to leave before something happens that neither of them can take back.

"Fine, Quon. I'll leave. Blazier, bring his stuff back in. I'll double your fee or rather *Quon* will since it's his money I'm paying you with."

The fury in Quon's face intensifies.

"You're not leaving me, Jané," he states in an adamant tone that makes her frightened of him for the first time since she met him.

"I didn't leave you. You left me. I'm just going along with the program," she reasons.

He steps forward.

"It's changed."

She steps back.

"No it's not. Get use to it," she says softly, determined to stand up for herself without pissing off Quon anymore than he is.

Blazier swivels his gaze to Jané.

"If you're ready to go, I'll walk you to your car."

She heaves a sigh of relief and has never been so glad to be rescued in her entire life. She is not sure what her husband will do next, and does not want to be around to find out either.

Quon turns sideways, balls his hand up, and let a fist fly right into Blazier's jaw. Jané screams then covers her mouth. Blazier staggers but recovers quickly then lifts a hand to his cheek already reddening. She starts to shake like a leaf caught in a hurricane, has never known Quon to hit anyone either. The other moving men rush around the house and stop at Blazier's backside. He is glaring at a furious Quon looking for a fight.

Blazier lets his hand drop then walks forward, taking up most of Quon's personal space before he stops moving.

"Mr. Sullivan, I know you're upset about losing your wife. I can understand that, but if you put another hand on her or me, you won't raise another one ever again. That's a promise," he vows too quietly. Jané believes him thoroughly and overcomes her horror in a hurry. She did not want anyone losing limbs or their job because of her.

"You need to leave, Quon, or I will have these men help *me* pack. I never thought you were capable of violence and was hoping there were no more sides to you that I haven't seen. I don't want to see anymore."

Quon advances on her before she can take her next breath. It takes no time for him to take up all three feet of her personal space or for her to guess that he really hates losing since he rarely does; accomplishing everything he sets his mind to.

"You're my wife, Jané. He can't have you," he declares in a guttural tone that sends blades of panic through every inch of her. She stares utterly shocked at him until a hand grabs her elbow and drags her backwards. A body has stepped between them before she realizes she is no longer looking at Quon, but Blazier's wide back. Only then does her stupefaction ease up on her nerves mercifully and gives her back a tiny fragment of her voice.

"I'm not your anything anymore, Quon," she asserts timidly, enormously relieved to have a barrier between her and him. Nor does she care that she is cowering behind Blazier as long as she is not facing her husband. Then, a hand appears behind Blazier's back. It is opened wide and searching for something. Jané yelps then stumbles backwards. The fingers grasp air for another second before vanishing. When Jané discerns that she has not been touched and the hand is really gone, she lifts her head to absorb the new commotion.

Blazier has Quon's shirt in two fists and trying to push him backwards. Quon has Blazier by the shoulders and trying to shove him in reverse. Neither man makes any headway with the other. She can barely believe what her eyes are seeing. Blazier's coworkers try to get in between the two men tussling, but neither wants to let go of the other. She stands completely stunned as the present becomes surreal to her.

How the hell did we get here?

"Let me go dammit! She's my wife," Quon screams. It takes all three moving men to shove him back the way they came.

Blazier yells back, "That's not how a man treats his wife or any woman! Brian, call the cops when you get his ass in the front yard!" Then, he begins to follow his coworker's progress with Quon up the sidewalk. Quon makes them work for it but they finally get him to the front of the house. Jané shakes her stupor when Blazier's command to call the cops sinks in. She did not want her husband here but not in trouble either. He is a good man when he is not cheating, understandably upset about the tides turning on his adulterous ass, and he did not hurt her, just Blazier who is being the bigger man about the situation once again. She, too, decides to be the better person and give Quon a choice; leave or deal with the cops.

"Wait," she yells then rushes behind the men moving swiftly to the front yard, with a furious Quon struggling all the way. She gets a glimpse of the surrounding neighbors occupying their front porches. It will not be long before the whole neighborhood comes to see what is going on. She makes comes a decision to use that to her advantage. Quon is anal about public opinion. She does not even want to think about how he will react if his reputation is ruined.

Jané slows down and steps cautiously towards a livid Quon then stops when she is within normal speaking distance. He stops struggling and just glares at her, like maybe he thinks this is all her fault. She does not give a damn what he thinks at this moment in time.

"Quon, calm down so we can talk like civilized people. Everyone is watching so if you do something stupid, they are going to call the police. You don't want that, do you?" she asks soothingly, hoping to manipulate his vanity and praying he does not figure that out. "Are you cool?"

After a moment of terse silence, he nods.

She exhales.

"Let him go, guys. Now come into the living room so we can talk, Quon." She decides that if it takes all night to convince him to move on, then she will talk *all* night. Before turning away to walk to her front door, she sends a wide-eyed glance to Blazier, hoping he understands that she needs him to stay close. He nods. She moves toward the entrance. Quon follows her. She stops in the entryway and palms the knob to support her trembling knees. She also did not want Quon shutting it or out any help she may need. She watches him walk through the living room to the kitchen, knowing better than to follow, planning to stay close to the exit, should he lose his cool again.

Blazier and his coworkers walk onto the front porch saddled with potted plants on wicker tables and matching rocking chairs. Nobody makes use of them. It is hard to get comfortable when you are waiting for hell to break loose again.

"Jané!" Quon bellows suddenly.

She flinches and glances at Blazier, who is fast becoming her tower of strength before answering, "Yes!"

"Come in the kitchen!"

"No, Quon! We talk in here or we don't at all," she retorts with a lot more conviction than she feels.

He steps into the doorway between the kitchen and living room.

"I *said* in the kitchen, Jané." His tone is hard, commanding, and rubbing her the wrong way.

"*I* said in here or nowhere. Take your pick," she tosses back softly.

He points to the men on the front porch.

"Oh you think they'll protect you?"

Jané takes the inquiry as a threat and starts to drift between frightened and furious.

"Protect me from what, Quon? You're going to hurt me now because I won't take you back for the same reason?" She still finds it hard to believe that this is the same man she has loved for years.

He squares his broad shoulders.

"Jané, come in here so we can talk *privately*," he demands a lot quieter. She figures he is not going to answer her question and thinks the time to cut off all communication between them has arrived.

Fuck Quon's reputation. It is not helping me in the slightest right now and I'm not risking my ass for it.

She turns to the group of men.

"Blazier, call the cops."

Quon rushes into the living room. Blazier takes a step forward. Quon stops when he stands over Jané, giving her a pitiful haggard look.

"Wait! I'll go but are we still going to dinner tonight?"

His audacity to think she wanted to be in his vicinity after he became violent has Jané doing a double take, and damn near giving herself whiplash.

"You have lost your damn mind if you think I'm going anywhere with you after today," she shrieks then quiets down. "I don't know you and I have learned more than I care to about the new *you*. You need to tell these men where to take your stuff and don't come back here."

Now that she knows he is capable of anything when he does not get his way, she intends to keep as much distance between them as possible. Cheating is one thing. Physical abuse is a whole other vicious animal and Quon has graduated to it.

His haggard look intensifies to a defeated glower. Jané becomes more than uneasy while bearing the weight of it.

"Did you ever love me?" he whispers suddenly.

She smiles sadly.

"More than my life, Quon," she murmurs back and becomes more convinced that she spent seven years making her husband into someone that he is not. This means the love between them was not lost or gone, but never real. Her heart fractures in the places it was not already broken. She does not bother asking him the same question he just asked her. There is every chance the answer will hurt her more than his affair ever could.

"Then why?" he asks softly, pulling at every one of Jané's heart strings again, but she cannot take him back.

"Because this is what you wanted. Because I don't think you want me, just don't want to lose me. Because I won't let you hurt me again. Because you're a sore loser and winner. Because—" she shuts up when she catches a glimpse of the clock. An hour has passed and she has totally forgotten about Simone.

"Quon, there are so many other reasons but we don't have time to discuss it. I have to be somewhere."

He frowns.

"Where are you going?"

"Out," she says quietly.

"*With who?*" he roars suddenly.

She yells right back, "Nunya! That means none of your business! Why can't you accept that is what I am to you now?"

"Because —" he bellows then trails off, wheeling his gaze to the group of men that seem to have moved closer without either of them realizing it. Blazier stands on the frontlines, giving her a peace of mind she has not known in months.

Quon looks down at her again.

"Look. I'll leave and call you later," he mumbles then walks off, forcing his way through the men to get to his car parked behind the moving truck. She assumes he came home...*here*...because she would not answer the phone, and remembers he never said where to take his stuff.

"Wait! What about your things?" she yells out of the doorway, not caring who hears. She is sticking firmly to not going anywhere near him.

He stops halfway to his car and pivots on his heels.

"They still go to the original destination, Jané, my *office*. I have an empty one they can store the boxes in." She finds that highly strange, and expected his belongings to be rerouted to the other woman's house. It nags at her that they are not going there.

Her curiosity gets the best of her and she finds herself yelling across the yard again.

"What about Marilyn's house?"

He grimaces.

"I told you. We're over."

"Just like that?" she asks before thinking, but could not have stopped herself even if she had thought about it first. She needs to know.

He nods.

"Just like that. She went too far when she called you a bitch. No one hurts or attacks you, Jané."

"Except you, huh?" she asks patronizingly.

He looks away then back like something is weighing heavily on him.

"I do love you, Jané."

He leaves another question unanswered.

She huffs, "I highly doubt that."

"Sometimes we hurt the ones we love, sweetheart, but I'm not giving up on us," he says softly, and tugs at her heart again. She has waited six months to hear those words and it takes every bit of strength she possesses to not run to him. She probably would have if she recognized the man she would be running to. Instead, she tightens her grip on the doorknob to ground herself.

"I'm sorry, Quon, but you should give up."

He does not reply but turns away and finishes crossing the yard to his car. She watches him speed away.

"What a fucking jerk!" the man with the gorgeous dreadlocks bellows suddenly. Jané takes a deep breath, suddenly feeling like she has taken too many hits of caffeine and does not know how to come down off the jittery high.

"I'm sorry, guys. He's never acted like that before. I don't know what got into him."

Blazier peers down at her.

"His regrets, when you told him to piss off. Now he's pissed off." The guys chuckle quietly behind him. She hopes she has not opened Pandora's Box and unleashed seven different hells on herself by not giving Quon a second chance, but she is not sure which Quon she will be getting. She could forgive, maybe even forget his trespasses against her heart, but she cannot be absolutely certain that the new Quon will not hurt her in some other way. She feels like she is worse off than she was before he asked for a divorce, and has no idea what to do about it. So, she looks to Blazier, the post-divorce guru.

"What do I do now?" she asks, stumped and afraid for her future, but not of it anymore. She wants it badly enough to ask anyone for advice on how to get it.

He lifts his hand and rests it on her shoulder, sending a little comfort to her frazzled nerves.

"Act accordingly. Keep an eye on your surroundings until this is over."

His coworkers grin then walk into the house as if they are trying to give them a moment alone. Jané finds that even stranger than Quon flipping the script on her. She watches them disappear up the stairs then turns back to Blazier.

"You think he'll hurt me?"

"I don't know what he'll do and you should expect anything. There might not be help around next time. He is hurting too now, even if it's just in his ego. It carries a lot of weight. Next time call the cops. You need to report his behavior and let people know that he is acting like this. Secrets can become your enemy at times like these." He takes his hand away to look at his watch. She recognizes it as Cartier, an expensive timepiece for movers and shakers. Blazier is just a mover.

He must move a lot of furniture.

He drops his wrist and looks down at her.

"I have to go, Jané. The guys went ahead and grabbed the boxes from your bedroom while you were speaking to your husband. Carlos left you an invoice for the load on your coffee table. My personal number is on it. Call if you need anything or for no reason at all. It was nice to meet you." Then, he grins and walks away before she can respond. She stares at his retreating back with her mouth opened wide. The rest of the men squeezes pass her body. She is too frozen with shock to move out of the doorway.

When the moving truck vanishes from her sight, she still stands in the doorway undecided if Blazier just came on to her or left the option on the table. Neither has she forgotten that she had not thanked or apologized to him for being her white knight today, but she will after she meets up with Simone. Thinking about talking to Blazier again brings a small smile to her face. Remembering she *has* to talk to Simone again makes her twirl around to check the clock on the wall. She has fifteen minutes to find Sensual Salon which could be anywhere in Tucson. She rushes to the alcove shielding her purse and keys, and extracts her phone from her pocket. She finds several texts and missed calls from Simone and Quon. She skips the calls and opens the text. Simone sent directions over an hour ago to an area about ten minutes away depending on the traffic. Jané moans about the five o'clock rush that will be just getting started, and certainly going to make her late.

Damn you, Quon.

She quickly punches in her code for the alarm by the front door and scampers out of it.

Simone will not believe the day I just had, Jané thinks as she reverses out of the front drive and speeds away. She even suspects Simone will be too shocked to be angry about Quon's bizarre behavior, Simone is angry about everything.

Chapter Six

With two minutes to spare, Jané barely finds a parking space near Simone's car and the spa in a one-level building with several more businesses on each side of it. All have tiny white letters that spell out each company's name and blend in with the paint on the doors.

How the hell did Simone find this place? She wonders as she shoves Sensual's entrance open. Simone jumps up from her seat and races to Jané, whose phone lights up in her hand.

Sullivan's Global again.

She ignores the call and shoves the phone back in her pocket. Simone reaches for a hug and Jané goes into her embrace willingly.

"I didn't think you were coming, Jané," she squeals.

She grins into Simone's slight shoulder. "You did promise to come pull me out of my house. I thought I'd save you the trouble."

A woman approaches them in a green uniform.

"Simone and Jané?" she asks too bubbly for Jané's taste. Simone steps back. They both nod at the employee who grins and extends both her hands for them to shake.

"I'm Lindsey. Welcome to Sensual's where there is no sin in the pleasure you will find here. If you're ready for your treatments, let's get your experience started," she chirps and clasps her hands together like she has won something.

Damn, Lindsey is hyper.

Standing next to the overly excited women with a mass of strawberry blond hair and matching body parts makes Jané feel downright plain. She is so ready for those treatments and happily follows Lindsey back to an enormous room lit with candles releasing pleasant aromas. Each corner of the area is sectioned off for different experiences.

Once they undress, Lindsey gives them a list of what to expect during their visit then calls in two hunks to start the massages. Simone jumps right into demanding details of Jané's life for the last half year and forbids any skimping on the details. Jané starts with last night's escapade into forbidden sex heaven and works her way backwards before ending with Quon's swift decline into madman's canyon. Simone's mouth drops open halfway through the conversation like she is in absolute distress but she says nothing.

At the end of their facial, mud bath, manicure, and pedicure, Simone still has not uttered a single word. Jané does not mind, at first. The peacefulness in the spa and unwinding in a neutral zone is doing wonders for her mental space overcrowded with things she thought she could not share to spare her marriage. It still stings that she got a divorce for her troubles.

By wash and condition time, Jané runs out of details and begins to enjoy herself immensely, not minding the quiet for the first time since Quon began breaking her heart. Being catered to along with Simone's company makes up for the lack of response in Simone.

Jané loosens up enough to slip into a relaxing doze where all her troubles and nightmares stay away, thankfully, until it's time for the next phase. They move silently to a table in the top corner of the room where she and Simone both come to regret the bikini wax instantly and cannot get back to the corner they started in fast enough. Then, Simone falls silent again. Jané takes more notice of her friend's odd hushed demeanor but says nothing, determined to enjoy this outing. But it starts to bother her that Simone has not asked a single question about why she hid her marriage woes from her. She is even surprised that Simone has not hit the roof about Quon's bizarre aggressiveness. Simone hates controlling men since her father was one. Finally during their hair experience, Simone begins to talk about her job. Jané comes to the conclusion that maybe she got *too* personal about her life and decides to not bring up it again.

After the stylist blow dries Jané's hair until it bounces around her like a thick curtain, she applies a light coat of foundation, mascara, and gloss to Jané's gleaming caramel skin, the last part of their experience. She redresses beside Simone, who has grown mute again. Jané is ready for a night out, but is not all that certain about her best friend who seems distant even when they return to the lobby to pay for their visit. Lindsey takes their money happily, of course. Simone grabs Jané's arm and ushers her out the door. They reach Jané's car first. Simone lets her go then walks into Jané's space. Simone's dark chocolate skin seems tight under her makeup. Her button nose is scrunched, and black eyes gleam like she is angry about something.

"I'm going to fucking kill him," she hisses suddenly. Jané leans back, stunned, and has no idea who her friend is talking about because she sure has hell did not want to talk about Jané's problems.

"Who, Simone?" Jane asks her then watches her plants her fists on her too thin hips.

"*Your* husband! I'm going to cut his balls off and mail them to his mama! I almost bust a gut in there trying to keep quiet and not scare those people half to death. Who is the bitch he is cheating with? She'll meet me in a dark alley before night fall and leave with a toe tag." Simone nods her head vigorously, emphasizing her point while plotting two murders in public. Jané knew better than to *not* take her seriously but starts to giggle anyway. For a moment, she thought her friend was regretting meeting her here today, but the crazy chick was actually trying to show some restraint. That is even funnier to Jané because self-control is the last thing Simone exercises.

Jané reaches up with one hand and squeezes Simone's shoulder.

"It doesn't matter who she is. She already has Quon and I'm working through my issues with it. From the way he went off today, she didn't get a prize but she's in for some *sur*prises if she doesn't cut him loose. I don't think she will though."

God bless the silly bitch.

Simone frowns.

"Serves her ass right too. Why do people screw someone else's spouse when they know they don't want someone screwing theirs?"

Jané hopes that question is rhetorical because she does not know the answer.

"I don't know but I had a damn fine time being the other woman last night and I didn't have to cook him breakfast this morning. But I didn't get out of making his coffee though." Then, she throws her head back and howls with laughter at her own twisted punch line.

Simone takes Jané's hand off her shoulder and closes it in hers.

"You're the wife. You can play whatever role you want with Quon. The other woman. A white woman. Submissive. Dominatrix. But she has no right to be anything to *your* man."

Reminding Jané that Quon is no longer hers makes her hilarity flee like there are hellhounds behind it. She allows herself to wallow in self-pity of going home alone which is ten times more agonizing than someone else's pity. So, she purposely remembers that Marilyn and Quon will have to reap what they sow one day even though he professes to have stopped cheating. Her self-pity lessens, but that relief from unburdening her troubles on Simone does not return.

Jané takes a shuddering breath.

"Marilyn had the right to do whatever she wanted to with Quon when he gave her the say so. It was his job to keep her out of our marriage. He didn't. Now it's over and he is no longer mine."

Simone simmers down.

"I'm still going to pop the bitch when I meet her. She could have done the right thing even if Quon didn't. She didn't *have* to be the other woman." She gives Jané a sympathetic look before saying, "Let's talk about something else. Now that we are beautiful, where are we going next?"

Jané has no idea.

"Hey don't look at me. I was a married twenty-five-year-old just yesterday and don't know what's hip anymore."

Simone snorts.

"*Hip?* You sound like you're eighteen."

Jané laughs and it feels damn good. She has not done that in six months.

"Fine! Where's the *hottest* club in Tucson?"

Her friend purses her lip as if she is thinking.

"There isn't one. Nobody wants dry Arizona grit sticking to their sweat when they come outside. But there's a nice lounge called Shadows on Forty-Fourth. Can you be ready by nine thirty and pick me up? Your car is the flashiest *and* the most reliable."

Jané starts to laugh even harder. Simone drives a beat up Altima that was probably the first car to come off the assembly line when Nissan opened its doors, and she hates it. Sometimes it breaks down, leaving Simone beside the road like it hates her, too.

When her giggles subside, she says, "Fine, Simone. I'll pick you up but I expect my dates to be ready on time. I want sex at the end of the night and no I am not buying you dinner first," she quips and gets a laugh out Simone, who waves her off.

"Whatever, girl, just don't stand me up or you won't get anything but a rock through your living room window. Haven't you heard? I'm nuts and I know where you live," she jokes. At least Jané hopes she is joking.

"Bye, Simone. Text me when you get home."

"Will do. Bye." Simone waves again and walks to her car. Jané drops into her navy blue leather seat, forgetting the phone in her pocket until it is pressing into her backside very uncomfortably. She shifts and retrieves it. It lights up in her hand immediately. Then Sullivan's Global violates the screen.

Jesus, Quon, you are turning into a damn stalker and if I don't answer, you will just keep calling. Shit!

Jané has to stop herself from pitching a conniption fit. She figures it will do her no good or stop him from calling. So, she taps the accept icon then hauls the cell resignedly to her ear.

"Yes."

"Is this Jané Sullivan?" a strange but familiar female's tone asks hushed but harshly. Jané immediately thinks it is Marilyn calling. But the first time she heard Quon's mistress talk, she was screaming and should not be calling from Quon's office or have her number.

I really hope he fired that bitch.

"This is her," Jané says warily then quickly develops a churning in her gut.

"Finally, you fucking answer. This is me, Marilyn Connor. The one your husband promised he would leave your ass for but *you* have to let him go first. He doesn't love you, Jané, so give him the damn divorce already," she orders viciously.

How many times has this bitch called me?

Jané bristles in the dry heat of the car that she forgot to crank and cool off. She does so now while gearing up to tell Marilyn where she could take a long walk off a short pier, and to stop calling her damn phone.

"Why do women always get confused with who to check when their relationship has hit a roadblock? I'm not your problem, Marilyn. *Quon* is. So why don't you harass him? And I've just been told to call the cops when I'm being bothered. You're bothering me. Don't *ever* call me again."

"Listen here, bitch! He's my man and I've waited for you to get use to that. I'm done waiting. Give him the damn divorce before he becomes a widower."

Jané's blood runs cold, not taking well to Marilyn's threat. She wishes immediately that she had recorded the call.

But how was I to know Quon's mistress would find my number and call me?

She begins to consider what all Quon's affair has brought into their lives, much more than another woman.

A damn psycho comes quickly to Jané's mind and she hopes the list does not get longer. Marilyn obviously has no problems destroying anything that stands in her way, if she can make a heinous threat over the phone with no fear of retaliation.

"Marilyn, you have to be the sorriest excuse for a woman if you have to step inside someone's marriage to have a man and then you're stupid enough to believe everything he tells—"

"Bitch, I didn't step inside! I was *flown* inside on a private jet. You—"

"No, you have what you want, bitch." Jané hurriedly cuts off Marilyn's goading, which is becoming to be a waking nightmare. "I gave it to you last night by agreeing to the divorce, moving Quon's shit out of my house, and going on with my life. He has been all yours for hours. Why don't you call him and ask why he didn't tell you because if you dial my number again, I will have a restraining order taken out on the both of you. You two have ruined my marriage and that's *all* you two are going to get." Jané removes the phone from her ear and punches the end call icon.

She regrets instantly not telling Marilyn about her and Quon screwing last night and how much he loved it. But, Marilyn is already in for a world of hurt. Quon is an even bigger cheating bastard than she thought to let Marilyn think that he had not moved on. Marilyn is welcome to become the wife that he betrays next. Jané gets a little closer to not caring if Quon marries someone else when it once tore her up inside to just think of him moving on without her. It only stings a bit now. Quon made the mistake of showing her sides to him she never knew existed. If he will conceal those from her for seven years, there is definitely more under the surface. Jané will happily leave Marilyn to discover those new layers for herself.

A tap on her window has her jumping in her seat, startled. She turns to find Simone frowning through the glass. She quickly presses the button to lower it.

"Jesus, Simone, you scared the hell out of me," she shrieks then tries to catch her breath that left for parts unknown without her.

Simone sniggers.

"Who was on the phone? I saw your face and knew something was up."

Jané twists in her seat to glare at Simone.

"Can you believe that was Quon's girlfriend calling to tell me to give him a divorce or she would make him a widower?" she asks with a heavy tone of disbelief.

Simone scowls.

"Make him a widower?" She waits a beat to ponder the words she'd mimicked like a parrot. Then, her eyes start to bulge out of her head. Jané knows exactly when Simone understands fully.

"Oh hell no! That bitch called you and threatened you! You *will* call the cops and right damn now, or *I* will. You can't let her get away with this!" As usual, Simone flies right off the handle.

"Simone, I am giving him a divorce so we don't have anything to worry about and I don't want to make 'he said, she said' reports to the cops if I call them. I want to present hard evidence. What I need to do is to call Quon, let him know his girlfriend is out of control, and find some recording devices for my phones. I'm not taking this lightly but I went to college for criminal justice, remember? Cops don't like to follow up on conversations you can't prove happened."

Simone grimaces.

"I hate when you're right. Now, what are we going to do?"

Jané frowns.

"We? I thought you had to go home and get ready?"

Simone pulls air through her teeth belligerently.

"Girl, I am not leaving you alone with those two nutcases roaming around free and hassling you when you will not call the cops. What you will do is call Quon right now and put him on speakerphone. I want to hear what he has to say when you tell him what's going on. You need witnesses for everything now just in case something happens."

Jané distinguishes truth in Simone's words almost unwillingly. She did not want anyone to know she was being dragged through more shit because of her marriage. It is embarrassing but witnesses are a big help when it comes to reporting events to cops who hate gossip and rumors. So, she dials Quon's cell, instead of his office. For all Jané knows, Marilyn will pick up the phone herself.

Hiss line rings twice before he answers out of breath.

"Jané, where in the hell have you been? I've been calling you since I left the house!" he bellows.

She sighs.

"I've been at a spa, Quon, though it's none of *your* concern but the reason I'm calling is. Your girlfriend just called me from your office talking about me divorcing you or making you a widower. I thought you said you fired her. Now how did she get my number?" Her tone is drenched in anger and suspicion.

She feels like Quon has been lying since they met and now about firing Marilyn. But she has to keep him in the loop of what is going on with his problem that is determined to land in her lap. It is not fair they ripped her world from under her and about to do the same to the new one she is trying to build around her out of nothing. Or rather she thought it was out of nothing until Marilyn called, threatening to topple it. Those unlimited possibilities that she is somewhat frightened of, suddenly becomes like icing on a cake; she wants them badly now no matter what it will do to her thighs. But two adulterous idiots have to get out of her way first.

Quon's responding sigh sails across the line and mutates like he is swiping a hand over his face tiredly.

"I tried to fire her, Jané, but she has an airtight contract as head of my advertising department. If she loses her job for any reason other than not performing her job or committing criminals acts in the workplace, I have to pay her a severance package of a million dollars."

Simone laughs out loud.

"And you signed the deal like an idiot *and* slept with the bitch. She's smart. I give her that much. Much smarter than you, Quon, it seems. But if she calls my girl one more time because you won't let her go, Marilyn will be a *dead* smart bitch and that's not a promise but a goddamn guarantee."

Jané starts to giggle under her breath. Simone is on ten already. She will be lighting a cigarette soon just to calm herself down. It seems like nothing else ever does. At this rate, Jané will be smoking right along with her.

"Is that...*Simone?*"Quon asks apprehensively.

Simone and Quon have not gotten along since Jané met her at a two-level mall in downtown Tucson four years ago right after she and Quon moved here. The two women clicked instantly. Jané brought her new friend home like a stray puppy. Simone and Quon have rubbed each other like sandpaper does wood, from the beginning. Neither ever comes out smooth in the end. What Jané cannot figure is out *why* they do not like each other.

Maybe Simone saw something in Quon I didn't and just didn't tell me, trying to spare my feelings.

As far as Jané is concerned, she is seeing too much now but she would love to know what keeps Simone at Quon's throat.

Then, Simone nods like he can see her.

"Yeah it's me. What else do you want to know?" she asks smartly.

He sighs.

"I know I did not miss that attitude." His response is dryer than a mouth after a hangover.

"From what I hear, you haven't missed anything on this side of the phone in a good while," she retorts.

"Jané, I don't have time for this childish shit so can we get to the point of the conversation," he counters indignantly. She is learning he does not have time for anything he does not want to face.

"The point is I would like to know how Marilyn got my number. If she calls me again, I'm reporting her to the cops and not sparing any details," she warns.

"You don't have to do that, Jané. I will handle her on this end and I'll call you as soon as I've spoken with her."

Simone crosses her arms and shifts her weight to one leg.

"Quon, you do know you can call the cops now right? Marilyn *is* harassing your soon-to-be-ex-wife from the company's phone. That's a crime and breach of contract. You can ask the officers to keep your affair with her and the report quiet, but give her a stern warning about contacting Jané again. You should keep a record of any phone calls she makes since you can't seem to fire her or say how she got Jané's number. But I have a pretty good idea how. It involves you leaving your phone unattended at some point, probably after you fucked her. I can promise you she's had the number for quite awhile, waiting to use it when she felt like she needed to rush your breakup along."

Jané agrees with Simone.

Marilyn has to be an intelligent woman to run a whole advertising department, and now she is tired of being in the background. Jané is certain that everyone at the company probably knows about the affair. Unfortunately for Jané, she is the one that Marilyn wants to be aware of it. She just wishes Marilyn would understand that *she* does not stand in the way of the main girl's spot in Quon's life. But she has a stomach roiling suspicion that Marilyn is just as selfish and hard of hearing as he is. Maybe even selfish enough to kill to get what she wants. That worries Jané a lot.

"Well thank you for that assessment, Detective Caslon," Quon says sarcastically. "Now can I talk to my wife without you butting in or are you her spokesperson now?"

Simone snorts then covers her mouth with a hand. Jané cannot help but laugh out loud rudely in his ear.

"Jané," he shouts into the phone. His obvious anger only makes them laugh harder at him. Jané would normally have loads of compassion for his world that is coming apart at the seams. He does not seem to be coping well. She knows how much he likes order. But she is realizing just how much he likes control, too. Apparently, that includes her. So, she does not feel compassionate towards him. Nothing is working out for either of them and he will have to deal with it just like she does.

"What?" she manages to ask through more peals of laughter.

"I'm glad you're finding all of this funny but we need to discuss dinner tonight," he shoots back belligerently, causing her to laugh more wildly. She cannot remember the last time she laughed like this.

"Are you serious, Quon? You still think I'm going out with you after you punched Blazier, and your mistress just called and threatened me? I want nothing to do with you *or* her. Why can't you have dinner with her? She's probably free since she's all wrapped in you."

"I want to have dinner with my wife not her," he says in a hostile tone, which is not convincing her to go. Her mirth simmers down when selfish Quon resurfaces. The violent one will probably follow. Neither cares about what anyone else's wants.

"Well I was going to stand you up, Quon, but I'll give you the courtesy of warning you. I'm not having dinner with you tonight or any other. You brought that psychopath into our lives and I want absolutely nothing to do with what she's after, that would be *you*. Now go deal with her and leave me alone. While you're at it, tell her to do the same. Please with a cherry on top. I'm only going to ask nicely this one time." She sees no reason to keep talking to him when he is not listening anyway. He has been warned that nothing is or will be right in his world again. So, she swipes the end call icon again.

Simone snickers.

"*You hung up on him,*" she squeals, shocked. Jané would not usually do something so childish, but he is bringing that side out of her.

"Yes I hung up. I've been doing it all day but he won't quit calling me."

"That's because you're being mean. When you treat most men like kings, they walk all over you. But take away their toys and put them in timeout, they love the very ground you're walking on."

Jané shakes her head, confused.

"That makes no sense."

Simone shrugs.

"It doesn't have to make sense. It just is. You accept it and move on. Now I can go home and get ready. I expect you at nine thirty sharp and I will be checking on you. If you miss one call or text, I'm coming over there in that damn clunker. Your neighbors will take one look at it being driven by a black woman and say "there goes the neighborhood". Avoid the humiliation and answer the phone."

Jané starts to snigger until she chokes, while nodding to Simone, who blows her a kiss and walks away.

Jané remembers to turn her ringer back on before she pulls out of the parking lot. On the way home, she wonders what is going through Marilyn's mind as Quon gives her a talking-to. Did he grab her by the shoulders tightly like he did Jané's to make Marilyn listen and submit? Is Marilyn making another scene for everyone in the office?

Marilyn does not seem the type to like being told what to do, more the bossy kind.

Quon has gotten us both into some deep shit.

She can even feel it overflowing into her shoes. She will not be taking her independence lightly once she gets free and clear of this *shit* either. As soon as she gets the chance, she plans to change the locks on the doors and the code to the alarm, but that does not mean he will stay away, especially when he refuses to believe Jané wants nothing to do with him anymore. She can even see him taking advantage of the easy access to regain his wife. But she does not want that to be regained by someone she does not know anymore. What scares her most about Quon is that he did not give one thought for his reputation or the other men witnessing the extra layers of his personality peel back like an onion, which reminds Jané that she has not called and thanked Blazier yet.

She lets her mind wander to the gentle giant that took a punch for her today. She does not care that he is just a mover. He is a good man that knows what it feels like to be taken for granted, and the least likely to do it to someone else. He definitely does not seem the type to abuse women and she likes that best about him. She gets the urge to call and tell him about the phone call from Marilyn, but he is probably still at work. She is not sure what time he gets off but hopes it is soon. Her urge to contact him is becoming almost too powerful to resist.

Just as she pulls into her garage, she orders herself to wait until after nine, making sure he is off. If he is not, she will try again in the morning, though she wants to hear his voice now. She has already discovered that it will soothe her and tell her what to do next in the same breath. But, she despises needing guidance into her new life that is already loaded with snags. This will be her first time living alone.

She smiles fondly when she remembers her aunt, Leora, who took her in for a few months after her parents died. Leora was the one to convince her that going off to college so soon after her parent's death is what they would have wanted. As much as she would have loved to just waste away in her aunt's house, she decided that her aunt was right and let Leora drive her to school, where she met Quon on her first day there. Even then, Jané had a roommate in a dorm room the size of a rat trap. But none of that would prepare her to deal with a man, and his lover promising to be just as or worst. It pushes her close to her breaking point that she has to now.

She still finds it shocking that Marilyn actually threatened her right along with wanting to tell a virtual stranger about it. Since she already has enough problems circling her like hungry wolves, she mentally skirts around the fact that the urge to call Blazier has everything to do with him saving her once and she might need it again, if Marilyn proves to be as dangerous as she sounds. But, she refuses to admit to herself that she is attracted to him. She just cannot handle that on top of everything else spiraling out of control.

So she denies it, drives into her garage, exits the car, and unlocks the door leading into the kitchen. She drops her purse down on the kitchen counter, exhumes the invoice with Blazier's number on it, positions her cell in her hand, and punches in the number written beautifully on bottom of the paper. She hesitates before swiping the send button, wondering if he will think it is creepy that she is calling with an update of her life like they are long-time friends.

He probably will.

She decides to not mention Marilyn, just thank him for keeping Quon's brand new controlling and abusive ass off hers.

She allows the call to go through, except Blazier does not answer. When the voicemail picks up and his baritone fills her ear, she shivers and smiles while listening to him prompt her to leave a message at the beep. She cannot help the tingling taking over her either and suddenly cannot avoid that she is attracted to him, which is bad. But she has no plans to act on the pull of the attraction to him. Not until she is disconnected from Quon lawfully. Then, she will fully move on without putting her heart into anything a man offers. Quon has broken that part of her.

"Hey, Blazier. It's me, Jané Sullivan. I wanted to call and thank you about mediating my husband's downward spiral into madness today. Oh and I'm sorry he hit you. I hope you're okay and give me a call so I know for sure. Well, bye." She did not know what else to say so she hangs up, checks the time on the phone then drops it beside her purse on the island. She has an hour and a half to shower and dress before picking up Simone.

She jogs up the stairs, her mind alternating between Blazier and what she wants to wear tonight. She quickly covers her hair in a cap and hops into the shower without touching her face, wanting to keep the makeup in perfect condition though she hardly ever wears it. Neither has she bothered at all with it since Quon started pushing her out of his life.

As she gets out the shower intending to brush her teeth, her stomach grumbles, cannot recall eating since this morning. She decides to remedy that after donning a black, satin robe that reaches her mid-thigh, and goes downstairs to find something quick before finishing preparing for tonight. When she enters the living room, a soft bump resonates from the kitchen just like the sound of the door to the garage closing. She stops dead in her tracks, was not expecting anyone, especially to come from the kitchen. Quon should still be at work. The alarm will be going off soon if he does not punch in the code for the alarm on garage remote. Seconds pass, the alarm does not go off. Quon does not enter the living room.

Her heart starts to pound in her chest. She has never had to deal with a burglar before and does not want to start now.

That's what the alarm is for. So why is it not going off?

Chapter Seven

She has had a few bad experiences with the siren loud enough to scare away Jesus when it is tripped after they had the last one replaced. A potential crook would be child's play to it, if it was working. Her eyes begin to roam the room looking for a weapon. They land on the alcove hiding the cordless phone. Another bump emanates in the kitchen this time. It jump starts her heart already in overdrive and her feet. She turns and runs for the only link to help.

"Jané!" someone shouts suddenly. She freezes inches away from the lifeline, screams, spins around, and realizes just how stupid a move that was before Quon walks into the living room. He stops and stands in the doorway between the rooms, and looks at her oddly. She has never been so glad to see him before now. Her hand flies to her chest where her heart is trying desperately to get out of.

"Dammit, Quon! You nearly gave me a heart attack and I almost called the cops on you," she shrieks, winded like she just run a marathon standing in place. Then, she remembers she told him never to come back here.

"What are you doing here?" she snaps, quickly becoming angry. He is turning into a problem that cannot seem to get that she no longer wants it around.

"I still have my key, Jané, and I live here. Or did you forget?" he replies stubbornly. She quietly declares this arrangement of her staying here while he still comes in and out as he pleases as impossible. Something must be done about it.

"You know what, Quon? I'm not even going to keep saying what you obviously aren't hearing. Fine! This is *your* house."

She plops down in the oversized, cream couch with brown, wide stripes and huge, cream Fleur de lis symbols sewn into them. She needs to catch her breath and stem the flood of fear still traipsing through her while deciding where she will live.

Quon takes a seat beside her.

"I know you don't want me here, Jané," he says softly, staring at the floor.

She turns her head slowly in his direction.

"Do you now? And yet you keep popping up. Do you know I couldn't get you to spend five minutes with me in the last six months?" she asks, condescendingly.

He sighs.

"Yeah I know. I was so caught up in me and what I wanted it never occurred to me I was hurting you." When he finally answers a question willing to be honest, she is taken aback, and swiftly plans to take full advantage of it.

"So now you're just going to make me want you after treating me like that?" Her tone is belligerent enough to make him look up at her desolately.

"I don't want to force you to take me back but I know you still love me. I figure if I come around enough you'll remember it too."

"Quon, I haven't forgotten how I feel about you but I don't want you back. Do you realize what type of monster you turned into today? You hit someone and you were gripping me way too tightly. You've never touched me like that before. I didn't recognize you and you scared the hell out of me acting that way." She summons up every second of his unusual behavior from today, and becomes even more leery of him.

"I admit I lost it completely. No, I don't act like that, but just the thought of you being with someone else kills me. If I promise to never do that again, will you give us a chance?" Then, he reaches for her hands resting in her lap. She allows him to hold them lightly in his and stare into her eyes pitifully. She cannot tell if he is sincere or just saying what he thinks she wants to hear. Although her heart goes out to him anyway, she is not a cruel woman by a long shot. But, she has heard enough about domestic violence to know that once it starts, it only gets worse. She declines to take that chance. She is a victim of his deceit already.

Isn't that enough?

Nevertheless, the thought of taking him back dances around her mind anyway. It worries her that she could even consider it. He may not be a budding wife beater. But what if she takes him back and he starts to believe she will forgive his every transgression?

That can't be the case anymore if he does hit women.

She loved him hard the first time so that he would never doubt her devotion to him and always made sure he knew she belonged to him heart and soul. But, Quon cannot care about that if he could crush her and their marriage beneath his heels without a second thought. She cannot forgive that. She does not want to, and slides her hands out of his slowly.

"Quon, there is more to you than meets the eye and I didn't like anything I saw today. Marilyn is a bigger problem than I originally thought but she's not mine to deal with. If I take you back, I don't think she'll just go away. I won't live with three people in my marriage again. You have to let me go," she begs.

God, what is it about this man that keeps me on my knees even when I'm sitting down?

He frowns.

"I can get rid of her for good. Just say the word, Jané, and I'll make it happen." His words collide with her mind like a bomb going off. Her eyebrows lift up until she thinks they are sitting on top of the widow's peak in the middle of her hairline. She does not want to believe that he is saying what she thinks he is, but she cannot mistake the tone of his voice for anything but what it is: a guarantee.

Shit! He just offered to kill for me.

Her Quon is not capable of murder. But this is not her Quon that she is sitting beside. Nor is he hers anymore. She asks herself if could this Quon and the one she that she thought she knew really kill for her, but decides not to ask either of them. She did not want to know, or risk becoming an unwilling accomplice to something she wants no part of. He will have to live with all the consequences of his actions from cheating with Marilyn.

"No, I don't want you to get rid of anyone. This is your mess, Quon. Just clean it up already and stop showing up here asking for me to take you back," she spits.

He drops his head into his hands. His elbows dig into his powerful thighs. Next, he runs his long fingers backwards through his hair. He has to be beyond upset to screw up the coating of natural waves that cover his skull. Quon buys as many products for his hair as women do for their faces. Both go completely overboard. Jané filled a box alone with them today.

Suddenly, his hands swan dives for hers again.

"Dammit, Jané, why can't you forgive me?" he asks in whisper rough with emotions, making her emotions come to the surface, too.

Her throat begins to burn as she says, "I did that for six months, Quon. Every time you didn't come home for lunch or dinner, I forgave you. The nights when you didn't call because you were with someone else and I knew it, I forgave. Even on the days you completely ignored me or gave an excuse why you couldn't bear to touch me, I forgave. When I could no longer deny you were having an affair, I forgave. But you hit someone today and now I'm all out of forgiveness. I won't let you do anything else to me."

A tear slips down her cheek quietly. She cannot push back the pain that threatens to choke her, as she admits something to herself she did not want to acknowledge ever; her life with Quon ended the minute he met Marilyn. She becomes sad that she survived the hell he put her through. Now, he will have to endure it too. But she does not think for a second that he will make it through because he is too selfish to let go of what is no longer his, her.

Jané gets the distinct impression she is about to enter into another hell of Quon's making if he does not acknowledge they are over, and soon.

Her looks up at Jané as more tears fall from her eyes then shift beside her, turning to gently wipe away the water on her cheeks with his thumbs.

"Don't cry, baby. I'll find a way to make this up to you. I know I fucked up, and I'm sorry. I'm *so*...sorry." His voice breaks. He hauls Jané into his arms where she breaks down completely into his chest, though he is probably the one looking for comfort. But the grief over her dead relationship has finally caught up with her and she needs the comfort more.

He holds her tightly until she quiets and comes up for air. The room is much darker than it was. She has no idea how long she cried. But, it cannot have been that long since the shadows of dusk were already filling the house when she came downstairs. She drops her head back on her neck to look up at him. His head falls forward until his lips are on hers. Her passion for him, that her heart has yet to abandon, wells up inside her. She knows she should stop him from kissing her after telling him they cannot be together anymore. He will be confused now and feel led on later when she tells him once again they will not relight the fire that used to blaze wildly in their marriage, except she needs the contact that comes with the kiss. She has always been a woman that needs to be touched, validating she is alive, and a woman that has been alone for too long. Once again, she decides to take what she wants though she will probably pay dearly for it afterwards.

He leans into her, gently pushing her down onto her back. She collapses with no protest, letting her hands clasp around his neck for aerial support. Her body feels weightless and she is not certain of how far down she has to go. His mouth is setting her insides on fire and sucking up all her oxygen, blowing her senses away. She has always loved that feeling. She even owns up to that she probably always will. Quon never fails to make sure she has all the satisfaction she can take, and then some.

His hands slips inside her robe. Her stomach clenches when his fingertips make contact with her breasts through the robe and rolls a dark nipple between his thumb and forefinger. At this moment, she is glad that he has always known just what to do when looking for a reaction from her. It does not fail this time either and she gives him one, moaning against his mouth. She cannot stifle her responses to his touch even if she wanted to. Quon is a born seducer and she loves that about him.

Jané also still loves when Quon's body is over hers. His thick muscular arms beside her head make a cocoon around her. This has always been her place of safety.

But who will protect me from him this time?

Blazier comes to mind immediately. She tosses the thought away before she can travel any further down that road. She will not start using him as the solution to her problems with Quon, and she has other needs that require a solution as well. She is going to let Quon supply it, and stops the all-consuming kiss to voice her demands.

"Take your clothes off, Quon."

He grins down at her, then shifts to his haunches to strip his body of his shoes then suit while she watches. She pulls the sash to her robe loose then separates the ends of it that meet in the middle of her chest. His smile widens as he drops one article of his clothing after another onto the floor.

"I love how bold you've become, Jané." His tone is throaty, an emotional indicator of the truth.

"Me too," she says simply. "Now come to me." She does not want to talk.

He leans over her. She mashes her lips to his to make sure he cannot utter another word then spreads her legs wide, silently directing him to where she wants him to be the most. He enters her without hesitation and begins to rock gently in and out. She starts to tremble, climb the stairs to an orgasmic paradise, and senses she will be riding the stars hard in no time, which is good. She does not want this to be an all-night love fest. For once, Jané is interested in a quickie. She does not require his time anymore, just his body.

Quon tunnels his hands underneath her body and lifts her up then crumples onto his back. She straddles him happily. His hips rise into hers at an unhurried thrust until he bottoms out on the upswing. Then, he sinks his hips into the couch, almost emptying her body of him completely, only to do rise and fill her all over again.

Jané begins a hushed mantra of his name put to the cadence of his movements, that push and pull her snug walls in whatever direction the base of his shaft is going. It makes his strokes endless and the sharp sensations of pleasure like a knife, cutting her mind wide open. She loses the ability to keep the chant of his name at a low volume, while she hovers like a helicopter over him. She starts to call out instead, along with her body, until neither can stand the continual bliss. It forces her to begin a rhythm of her own just to endure it: up and down then grind against his pelvis. This is where she makes the mistake of stimulating her clit against the short stubs of his hair. Her song becomes one loud note that lasts until her breath runs out. He groans. She smiles down on him. His hands wrap around her waist and gently guides her to where she first started, on her back. Then, he leans down and touches his nose to hers adoringly.

"Oh no you don't, Jané. You will not run this show too," he warns then sets his original pace again. But that will not do for her.

"Faster, Quon," she whispers before shifting upwards to nip at his earlobe and put a race in his pace. He curses then speeds up, giving a runaway train a run for its money. The crown of her head begins to rebound against the arm of the couch. The roughness of the sex quickly grows on her. Quon grins as if he likes giving her what she wants again. But she refuses to be caught up in the moment and taking things from it that could get her hurt again. Instead, she tightens her inner muscles in a rhythmic clench and release around his erection pillaging her body until they both go over the edge at the same time. The uncoordinated chirps of an alarm sound off in the far distance.

He collapses on top of her and starts a quiet chant of her name into her chest as she hones in on the noise that seems to be a lot closer than she originally thought, and sounding like it is coming from their garage. She knows both of their cars are in it because Quon came from the kitchen.

If he parked in the garage, he is not going to be leaving right away.

She is also pretty confident that he intends to stay for as long as it takes him to convince her to take him back, and probably not going to leave until that happens. But that is not her most pressing problem right now. What she cannot figure out is which car is requesting an audience.

She pushes the haze of their post-lovemaking away to concentrate on just how close the blaring really is. The notes of their car's alarm that should be a single chirp repeating seem to be running over each other instead. She quickly becomes certain the noise is coming from the garage and both cars are acting out. The fear she felt earlier, of someone being in the house that should not be, returns. She panics.

"Quon, get up!"

She pushes at his wide shoulders when he does not move faster. Only then does he lift his body to his hands still braced beside her head and looks down at her strangely again. Suddenly, he jerks his head toward the wall connected to the carport. Then he jumps up, scrambling to put on his pants. Jané pulls the rims of her robe together before finding her feet, to run into the kitchen and open the door that gives instant access to their vehicles. The noise is extremely loud with both car alarms simultaneously splitting the air wide in the closed space. Suddenly, Quon is behind her and the blaring stops. She looks back. He has both key rings in his hand.

She turns back around and examines the cars from the short staircase, afraid to go down into the garage now seeming like a semi-dark pit that could still be shielding the vandal in the inky black shadows. She looks toward the garage's door. It is closed but not resting completely on the ground like it should be, letting tiny trails of fading light creep under it. She and Quon always make it a point to remotely close it fully behind them after parking.

She starts to take inventory of the cars. Quon's seems to be fine from her vantage point overlooking the tops of them. As her eyes adjust to the dark, she realizes her sedan sits several inches lower when it should not. Immediately, she concludes that her tires have been slashed just before detecting a huge dent in her hood. Bitch is written in red bubble letters across the cracked windshield and she can see straight through the interior to the opposite wall housing Quon's tools. Jané loses her ability to breathe as she becomes aware that every one of her side windows must be somewhere else.

They are probably broken because they were all rolled up tight and intact when I got out of the car.

She begins to reluctantly absorb the proof that she has been targeted, and immediately hates the startling clarity of her mind. It is blown wide open with shock and awe which only seems to allow more unwanted facts to settle cerebrally. The person that committed this crime set off the alarms on purpose to get her attention.

Well they have it.

Then, she covers her mouth quickly with both hands to prevent a scream from getting free.

"My car," she whispers behind her fingers, before stepping down to follow the trio of stairs into the garage with one tiny bulb shining over both vehicles. She wants to look for any damage she cannot see from the doorway, but Quon shifts from behind her to beside her first. His arm wraps around her waist like a boa constrictor and hauls her backwards into his hard body before she completes the first step down. Then, he bends and slips his empty arm behind her knees, forces them to bend then lifts her up. She tumbles into his hard chest.

Damn, I couldn't pay this man to touch me before last night. Now he won't stop.

"You can't walk down there, Jané. You're barefoot and there's probably glass everywhere," he chastises and carries her back inside the house before setting her down on her feet in the doorway between the kitchen and living room. She stands there trembling violently while watching him sink to the couch to put his shoes back on.

"Who would do—" She starts, speaking muffled around her hands, but let her words trail off when her mind presents her with the upsetting answer before she can finish asking the question.

Marilyn. She is only one person with a reason to do this.

Jané starts to glare at Quon as more rage consumes her until she is choking on it.

She points a damning finger at him and begins to yell, "This is your fault! If you hadn't started messing with that psycho bitch, we wouldn't be going through all of this! Why did you have to screw up every damn thing by screwing her?"

He stops tying his shoes to peer guiltily at her.

"I'm sorry, Jané. I didn't know she was nuts."

Her eyes widen until she feels like her pupils will pop right off her head from the pressure.

"So if you could have proven she was crazy, you wouldn't have brought her to Arizona?" she asks sarcastically. But more questions push into her mind that did not occur to her last night, until her head feels like its swelling from the overload.

"How stupid could you be to have a damn affair, Quon? How many have you had?" Jané needs the answers more than her next breath.

He looks away.

She takes a livid step forward.

"How many? I deserve to know, you bastard!" she insists, knowing she is losing it big time but does not care. His actions are coming back to haunt them both and she hated it, and him, too.

Still he does not answer which only amps up her fury.

"*Tell* me," she hisses between clenched teeth.

He exhales then murmurs, "I've never *stopped* cheating. I was with someone when I met you."

Senseless rage for his deliberate actions and her mistake in marrying him rises in Jané's chest, rendering her speechless.

I married a goddamn serial cheater. A killer would have been better.

Jané starts to spin out mentally, not able to handle anymore answers from Quon's mouth. But that does not stop the questions from coming.

How many women has he had while with her? Why did he marry her out of all of them and expose her to more than just their jealousy and viciousness?

Neither can she can understand why he needs so many bodies beneath his nor asks. He cannot care for anyone but himself if he could do this. To hear him explain how much he does not care would probably kill her dead on the spot. Jané does not want to die. What she wants to do is hurl something and hurt Quon. She decides to do both at one time.

Her eyes begin to roam the room. Quon will be the one that needs the lifeline this time. The first projectile she spies is huge brown lamps with cream shades on glass end tables, sitting on both sides of the couch. She charges across the room for the closest one on his left. He jumps to his feet. She does not doubt that he is sensing his life is in danger. She reaches for the lamp and circles the base of it with a hand shaking with fury.

Quon's huge paw encircles hers before she lifts it.

"Don't, sweetheart. We need to call the police and report this. I know I was stupid and have no excuse for ruining your life but let me prove I can make it better," he pleads but he can quit talking now. Jané does not want to hear anything coming out of his mouth.

"You can't make this better. Marilyn has a mind of her own and unless it is separated it from her body we're stuck dealing with whatever she does next because you're a damn disgrace to black men everywhere. I *hate* you, Quon, and you're right. We're going to call the cops and tell them everything. Then I'm moving out and you had better not come anywhere near me. The first time that bitch finds me, you better be on her ass to stop her from doing one more thing to me," she snaps, then snatches her hand from under his, disgusted with his touch. She rushes across the room to retrieve the cordless and dial 911.

It makes her even angrier that she has to report what happened to her car when she knows for a fact that the cops will treat the vandalism as a 'he said, she said, and now I think' incident. There will be no proof that Marilyn broke multiple laws while they lay only feet away making love. But telling the police about Quon's affair will certainly point the finger in Marilyn's direction. Jané's contempt for them both grows as she waits for an operator to pick up the line.

After giving their information to a dispatcher, she cannot stomach the sight of Quon so she flees to the bedroom where she dresses and waits for officers to arrive, while fuming inside. He did not just destroy her life; he made her feel like a naïve idiot while he was doing it behind her back. She belittles herself for wearing rose-colored glasses and thinking her life was almost perfect. Maybe Quon wanted it to seem that way to her. Whatever the reason she lived so blindly, all of his chickens are coming home to roost in the middle of her denial-free world, and she wishes she did not see those either.

He respects Jané's need for distance and leaves her alone upstairs where she yearns for someone to talk to beside the man she is coming to dislike for sticking her in this situation. Simone comes to mind. Then, Blazier follows right behind, except he has not called her back. She does not want him to think that she is infatuated with him. Though she knows she is rapidly heading in that direction, one obsessed female in her life is enough.

Even if she wants to call Blazier, her cell is downstairs with Quon. She doubts if he will give her the privacy to call anybody. She does not want him to know that she is connecting with any man besides him, even after his heartbreaking admission downstairs. Though she thinks her husband does not deserve her respect anymore, there may not be any connection to make if Blazier never calls her back.

Jané has mixed feelings about not talking to him again, and knows she is in even more trouble than she thought when it comes to the beautiful blond mover. Her attraction is going to prove fatal to her vows if she does not keep a close watch on herself. Quon's disregard for his vows makes it difficult for her to want to keep an eye on anything. It is becoming even harder to not cheat as Quon did, just to hurt him. She starts to worry what she will do if Blazier shows even the smallest amount of interest in her. Her worry is a dead giveaway that she will not think twice about sleeping with him if he does. Nor is she in the right mind to care much about promises made before God or being the bigger person in her shattered relationship. There is nothing she can do that will make her feel bad after all that Quon has done, not even letting Blazier have her body in any way he wants. As far as Jané is concerned, her body is only attached to Quon's by a piece of paper and her own heartstrings. But, she needs to talk to someone that has not betrayed her in the last twenty-four hours.

And I cannot do any more damage to my marriage by having a damn conversation with a phone between me and one of the finest men I have met.

Jané makes up her mind to make that call whether Quon is here or not.

"Jané, the cops are here!" he shouts up the stairs just as she leaves the bed to retrieve her cell, making her have to wait to call Blazier. She gets extremely irritated about it.

"*I'm coming,*" she yells back then hisses, "Jerk."

When she tops the staircase leading directly to the front door, she finds two cops waiting on the porch below. Lighting from the same two lamps she wanted to throw at Quon's head, brushes their faces softly. Quon waits at the bottom of the stairs. When she reaches the last step, he extends a hand to her. She swats it away and sends him a nasty glance before halting in front of the officers, one black, one white.

Isn't it always that way these days?

Sometimes Jané thinks those are the only two races in America, often paired together to present a show of unity, just as Quon is trying to do for the officers. But he should have known better than to try that when he just told her that he is sleeping with everything not nailed down. She has no intentions of sparing that detail in her report to the cops, who are sending questionable looks her way. She realizes it probably was not the best decision on her part to show how angry she is with her husband. But she could not help it and is not playing the role of happy wife to satisfy anyone, especially when she loved her car more than ever now. She even has the title to it in her name. Quon insisted on that himself. Just when the car is not usable, it starts to represent the only thing he did not fake in their life together and the only way to leave their suburban home quickly turning into a waking nightmare for her,.

Ain't that a bitch?

Before now, Jané could not have cared less that she was being absorbed into Quon's life and depended on him solely because it was supposed to have been *their* life. Now, she feels like she is a part of a 'come one, come all' existence, and she wants no part in it.

She takes a deep breath before saying, "Hello, officers." They both nod then look away as if they move like Siamese twins often. The black cop whips out a skinny, black leather-bound notebook and pen from his breast pocket then sits his eyes down on a blank page.

The other officer stares pensively at her for a moment before asking, "What happened, ma'am?" His tone is dry and clipped, making her feel like she is a nuisance caller.

Jané is not sure which officer's conduct she dislikes more; the one that will not look at her or the one that seems the least interested in her problem. She feels shut down before she can even explain why they are here. Immediately, she thinks when she swatted at Quon, they jumped to conclusions and decided this is one of those pesky, domestic disputes that never get resolved no matter how much cops get involved. Had they bothered to reserve their judgment, both officers might actually be able to understand why she pushed Quon away.

But isn't that the way of America? Judge the book by its cover without taking a look inside first.

Now, Jané sees no point in talking to them.

"Why don't you two talk to my husband since you're both obviously irritated with me on his behalf," she says nastily then walks away to sit on the couch with her back ramrod straight. She begins to stare at the entertainment center in front of her without actually seeing it.

"Jané," Quon hisses from the doorway.

She does not bother turning her head to acknowledge him.

"Quon, you may not remember what classes I took in college but I can tell you exactly what those two are thinking. I won't get any help from them but you will. Now tell them why they're here so they'll stop thinking you and I are the problem." Her words are just as cynical as the officers who begin to fidget, shifting their lean weight from one side to the other after she called them out. She is probably irritating them even more. She does not care.

They will either help me with my Marilyn problem or they won't.

Chapter Eight

The cop that took the instant attitude with Jané, props a foot on the raised step up of the doorway.

"Ma'am, if you don't mind, I'd like for you to tell me what happened so Officer Tanner can take the report. He's real good with shorthand. Talk as fast as you need to," he requests with a curious tone. However, Jané is not in the mood to comply.

"No thanks. You *guys* have at it."

He huffs loudly from the doorway.

"We have to talk to you anyway since you live in the home. Might as well get it over with then you can be angry with us uninterrupted for jumping to conclusions. I'm Officer Peterson by the way."

Jané considers telling Tanner and Peterson to piss off, but Marilyn already felt pissed on and is probably not going away anytime soon. She decides to talk to the officer. He may be the only one who can get Marilyn off her back. She leaves her seat to rejoin them at the door.

"I arrived home from the spa about half an hour before Quon did, after getting a call from his girlfriend threatening to make him a widower if I didn't give him a divorce. I told her I'd already agreed to one and moved him out earlier today. I came home ten minutes later and took a shower. Quon arrived here just as I got out. We had sex in the living room. When it was over, I heard the alarms on both cars going off. We went to the garage where I realized only my car had been vandalized. I'm not exactly sure when it happened. My car must've been fine when he got here because he didn't say anything. Then we called you." Then Jané walks away, leaving Tanner to scribble furiously in his book.

Peterson is looking at her strangely as she resumes her seat.

"What's the name of the girlfriend?" he asks with a frown marring his tanned features.

Jané points at Quon.

"Ask him. She's *his* mistress."

Quon flinches then looks pathetically at her before giving the officers his undivided attention. Jané drops the pointer she would have gladly exchanged for her middle finger if she was thirteen years old. Instead, she tunes the men out and drifts deliberately into a mental nothingness while they thoroughly question Quon.

"Jané," Quon yells her name suddenly. She focuses on his concerned face, and realizes he could have called her any number of times before she heard him.

"What?" she answers with a bite.

He exhales loudly.

"They need us to go with them to the garage."

An image of Jané's damaged car flashes through her mind. Her eyes begin to burn. She knows right then that if she did not get herself under control, she would be drowning in tears again. She orders her mind to stop thinking about her only mode of transportation being the victim of a one-woman wrecking crew, and begins to breathe in and out deeply. But even if she manages to get her emotions in check, she does not want to go into that garage.

"Why can't you all just go? I don't want to see my car like that again," she mumbles, still working on salvaging her composure that does not want to be salvaged.

"Mrs. Sullivan," Peterson summons, "You have to identify which car is yours and we may have more questions to ask. I know we're not your favorite people right now but you have to help us do our job." But, she does not want to help them do anything, already knowing the outcome of their visit; they will not find evidence of Marilyn's visit. Afterwards, they will type up a report then leave it to rot in their database.

Marilyn may have been brave enough to break in here but I highly doubt that she will want anyone but me to know that.

Still, Jané decides to go through the motions. She has to if she wants that restraining order, and it looks like she is going to need it.

"Fine," she grumbles then leaves her seat to walk at a fast clip toward the front door. The officers spread apart so she can pass. She intends to take the same path as Marilyn would have and work her way inside the garage just like she did.

Jané enters the front yard then takes a left before strolling towards the garage. She and the cops both start to search the ground for signs of footprints along the way. But, there is grass between the front porch and concrete drive. She suspects that unless Marilyn wore shoes with heels to leave indentations in the soil and break the grass blades, or left impressions of her shoes on the pavement, they will not find a trail, and they do not.

She finally steps onto the strip of pavement leading into the garage, and notices her brake lights are resting on the ground along with chunks of her windows. Red letters spell get out slut across her back windshield. If Jané did not know better, she would think she is the home wrecker being hounded by someone's wife.

She turns slowly around until she is facing Quon, who looks like he would give every cent he has to be somewhere else right now.

"Jané—"

She swipes a hand through the air.

"Don't say you're sorry. It helps nothing," she whispers through gritted teeth and a sudden sheen of tears then turns away, pondering why Marilyn still chose to do this after being told she had gotten what she wanted. It only makes Marilyn's actions look even more senseless to Jané, who wants them to make sense badly.

"What is it, Mrs. Sullivan?" Peterson asks.

She realizes she is frowning, giving away her pensive state.

"I told Marilyn the divorce was coming. I sent Quon's things away. So why come here and do this? How does she know where I live? Why not target the house? How does she know that the car is the only thing I really own? Why hit me there next?" Jané's voice is barely audible as her mind plays with then tosses the questions out of her mouth.

Where did this bitch get her fucking information from?

She turns and looks at Quon. He is the only common denominator and an unlimited source of information for the other woman to tap into.

This bastard is guilty of far more than cheating.

Jané's is not only a victim of Quon's bad actions but Marilyn too. The other woman's knowledge could be limitless thanks to him.

All because of his loose damn lips, my ship is all but fucking sunk.

Nor is she convinced there is a great distance between it and the ocean floor at this point.

More tears slip from her eyes as his betrayals grow. She glowers at him.

"How much have you told her about me?"

He crosses his arms defensively.

"Jané—"

"Just answer the damn question. I don't want half-truths or lip service from you right now. This freak means business and it's time you stop with the front that you're a good guy before you *get me killed*," she finishes in a yell.

Peterson steps between them.

"Mrs. Sullivan, Officer Tanner will take you inside to calm down while I talk to your husband about this Marilyn."

Tanner does not dispute Peterson's order. Jané is not even sure if he can talk, but he is welcome to wait in her house without her because she is not going anywhere.

"Officer Peterson, you wanted me out here. I'm here. You and I both know this case won't make it pass your desk until someone is dead or hurt. That leaves me to find out why this happened before that happens."

Jané returns her full attention to her husband again.

"What did you tell her about me, Quon?"

He starts to move restlessly under her hostile glare before finally saying, "Everything."

"Everything!" she shrieks in utter disbelief that he could be so stupid for such a smart businessman.

I guess his senses come off with his pants. I'm shocked the bastard could even remember I existed when he was with her.

"You were our favorite topic, Jané," he confesses quietly.

"More like *hers*, you fucking idiot!"

Jané suddenly feels very unsafe in her own home. She does not know how much more access Marilyn has to it and her, besides her phone number and the garage.

The bitch probably has a key too. I'm being run out of my own home and I'm so fucking glad to go.

She and it both have been violated by a scorned woman who seems to be getting more and more psychotic by the second. Nor can she be sure that Marilyn has not been tracking her movements the whole time Quon has been sleeping with her, learning things about Jané for herself.

Jané does not see a way to protect herself adequately from Marilyn, when the other woman already knows so much about her.

"Mrs. Sullivan, go in the house. We'll take it from here." Peterson demands in a steely voice, brokering no arguments. Jané decides following his command is for the best since he has the iron bracelets and the right to take away her freedom, or rather what little Marilyn has left her with.

She sets her angry sights back on the man that gave Marilyn the power to take almost everything away from her.

"I hope turning your marriage into a damn free for all was worth it," she spews before pivoting on her heels and walking away without waiting for Tanner to catch up.

During her walk of humiliation, it nearly rips her apart inside to accept that she was never really Quon's wife, more like his bottom bitch with a little rank because of a marriage certificate. It infuriates her that she bore all the burdens of their relationship for a just a slice of his time.

But I was a damn good bottom bitch and he will regret losing me for an educated petty criminal.

Jané's head becomes a steel cage, trapping inside it every possible reason that Marilyn could successfully pull this crime off without them being the wiser of her proximity. Her mind settles on Marilyn possibly following Quon home, overhearing them making love, and made Jané's car pay the price. Jané is not the quietest of lovers. Now she has to worry about where she will live and how she will get there, quietly.

Simone enters her mind like a strike of lightning, a friend and ride rolled into one. Jané rushes through the front door, intending to reach the kitchen and retrieve her cell from beside her purse, but it is not there. She dives inside her handbag, finds it on the top of her wallet, and freezes in place, wondering why she found it there. She never puts it in her purse because its contents always manage to unlock the phone and dial out or send blank texts to no one in particular. Her purse has never been picky about who it reaches out to.

The only one who could have handled her phone is Quon while she was either showering or waiting for the cops upstairs. Then, she is certain that it was neither time. He was looking through her phone while she was wondering was there a burglar in the house, which is why it took him so long to enter the living room.

What the hell was he looking for? And I have never gone through his phone as much as I thought about it.

The phone rings in her hand, curtailing her thoughts. She eyeballs the screen, expecting Simone to be reaching out with a cautionary message in one form or another to tell Jané that it is getting close to the time to pick her up. Or Simone would show up raising enough hell to make the devil concerned. Since Jané has no transportation, their night out is now off and she does not feel like going out anymore anyway, but going away from here is a must. She still has to tell Simone that, and hopes Simone's car will bring her here.

As soon as Jané discovers it is just a text coming through from her cell company, the screen migrates to the incoming call display. A familiar number pops up with no name. But, her mind cannot recall where she should know the digits from. She frowns, knowing it could be Marilyn, and accepts the call hoping somewhat that it is. Jané does not care much for confrontation but she has a thing or three she wants to tell the bitch about working over her vehicle.

"Hello," she forces into the line.

"Jané, it's Blazier."

When she realizes it is just the blond mover that moves around her head a lot, she lifts her face skyward and blows relief all the way to heaven.

Thank you, God.

Then, she shoves the phone to her ear.

"Hey, Blazier." She says breathlessly, and cringes when she hears her desperate tone.

"What's wrong?" his deep timbre becomes worried.

She snorts.

"What's *not* wrong? My car has been demolished and written on by a woman with a grudge she should not have. I just found out my husband is a pimp that keeps all the ass for himself. But I'm the only ass he felt the need to lock down in a fraud marriage after he used it to cheat on someone else with. Other than that everything is fine," she jests. "Oh, and I was threatened today by Quon's mistress or one of them. I'm not sure how many he transported here just like he did me."

Jané would normally be worried about her dirty laundry being aired, except it is coming out anyway. She feels like she might as well be the one to make it available for public consumption since it is hers.

"What do you need the most right now, Jané?" he asks quietly, and adding fuel to her desire for him. He cares and that is what she needs the most, but she cannot tell him that.

"To get as far away from here as possible except I have no car. I don't even know if I can have it towed this late at night or find a rental company to lease one from. But I was just about to call my friend to come get me."

"Don't! I'll come take you where you want to go," he replies swiftly. Jané balks at his suggestion while secretly loving that he did offer. It is the only bright light in her dark world right now. However, she is adamant that their friendship or whatever it is that is developing between them will not start off with her being a burden on another man. Quon has already mistaken her for one. She refuses to let that happen again, especially with someone one she just met.

"Thanks but no, Blazier. I don't want you going out of your way to help me. You did that once today and I need to call—"

"Jané, stop. I haven't said or done anything I wouldn't for someone else in trouble and scared. You're both. I can hear it in your voice and I am only ten minutes away. Accept the ride and make me feel better about your situation," he implores.

Well someone should feel better about this shit storm because I sure as hell don't.

Yet, she feels guilty about making a stranger worry about her when she only wanted to vent, although Blazier is not a stranger anymore. He has been privy to her troubles as fast as she is learning they exist, and she wants to be in his company at least for a little while. But, it worries her that she may be trying to replace Quon too soon without realizing it. A big strong man to lean on is something she loves having, and Jané hates to be alone. But if she is aware of the problem, she can prevent it from becoming a bigger one.

"Okay, Blazier. I need to pack a bag and see if the cops have any more questions for me. Give me fifteen minutes. Tap the horn when you're outside."

"See you then, Jané. Bye."

She hangs up. Simone needs to be told about the latest episode preventing Jané from moving on in any way with her life. It bothers her that Simone has not made contact first. Simone should have shown up by now.

Jané searches through her contacts for her friend's number while blindly turning to go upstairs. She walks into another body first, a chest specifically. She almost drops her cell as momentum propels it and her backwards. She catches the phone in her chest and her balance by dropping one foot back on the tiled floor then glances up as hands seize her arms, steadying her. Quon is the solid mass that has stopped all progression again, and has hard dark orbs trained on her face.

"Who were you talking to, Jané? Where are you going? *Who* is coming here?" He forces the questions through clenched teeth, making her wonder how long he has been standing there. Fear of the man that she no longer recognizes, slithers down her spine.

"Everything okay?" Officer Peterson asks suddenly from behind Quon. Jané is relieved that she is not alone with her husband anymore.

"Ah…yes, officer. Is there anything else you need before I leave for the night? And can you stay until I go?" she asks throatily while being sucked into Quon's furious glare. His hands fall away like she hoped they would after issuing the silent threat.

Peterson looks at them both warily.

"We can do that, Mrs. Sullivan. How long will it take your ride to arrive?"

"I asked for fifteen minutes to pack a bag, but I can make it two if you need me to," she says hurriedly then steps around Quon. His stare gets sharper, piercing her flesh like needles, provoking her to take the stairs two at a time to her bedroom. As soon as she enters the closet, the bedroom door slams shut. She pauses as more dread swamps her.

"Jané," Quon calls softly, but the anger drenching his tone screams at her to get out now. But wherever she goes, she would like to be able to change clothes later, and does not believe Quon can do much with the cops waiting for her to leave.

She reaches up to the shelf above her dresses for a zebra print duffel bag, a Christmas gift from Matilda. Jané has never had cause to use it until now, but damn glad it is available when cause arrived. She starts grabbing jeans and shirts off hangers, stuffing them in the bag along with a pair of sneakers. She does not care that their dirty bottoms are on top of her clean clothes.

A sudden knock on the bedroom door startles her again. She freezes in place but allows her eyes to swivel toward the closet's opening and finds Quon standing in the doorway with both hands resting on the walls on each side of him. She regrets wanting to pack now that Quon's body blocks the only way out of there. His jaw starts to clench and release, eyes become suspiciously bright. He looks away quickly like he does not want her to see him lose control of his emotions.

"Jané, don't leave." His request is a whisper filled with misery. Then, his sad gaze returns to hers. Sympathy rises like a tidal wave in her chest, but his and her misery is his doing. It is his time to lose everything that he did not hold dear, and Jané does not want to block Karma from having her due. But, Karma is not going to make Quon move.

Jané washes her forehead with an exhausted swipe of her hand, trying to think of what to say to get Quon out of her way when another knock reverberates through the room, more insistent than the last.

"Mrs. and Mr. Sullivan, open the door now," Peterson orders.

Quon glances back at the door then at Jané again.

"Please, don't go, sweetheart."

She shakes her head.

"Quon, I'm not safe here because of you or with you. Now let me go and open the door please," she begs unashamedly. If she thought doing it on her knees would get her out of here, she would drop to them, gladly.

He takes a step forward.

"I know that, baby, and I'm trying to fix it but you have to stay to let me. Please for heaven's sake *let* me."

Jané dislikes his desperation immediately, though she can even relate to how he felt. Just last night, it was her being this frantic to get him to stay. But it will do him the same amount of good it did her, none.

"I don't have to *let* you do anything anymore, Quon. This time you will do all the letting and that means letting me leave," she whispers.

"I can't lose you, Jané," he whispers right back. A vicious banging slams through the quiet, making them both flinch.

"Open the door or we will knock it down, Mr. Sullivan." Peterson shouts. When Quon does not move to do as the officer says, Jané begins to panic right out of her mind. He is effectively holding her hostage.

"Quon, you did not lose me. You threw me away. There is a difference. You can't treat people like shit and expect them to always be around. I'm already gone in my mind. Can't you see that?"

His face transforms to an angry mask. He opens his pinched mouth to yell, "Then why did you make love to me twice, Jané, if you're already gone?"

She cringes then steps further back into the closet until she is draped in his clothes hanging up. She finds it unfair that taking what she wanted from him is already haunting her, when it took years for him to have to pay up. Now, she wishes the cops would just break the door down just as fast as her bill came due for making love to her husband. But, since that does not look like it is going to happen any time soon, she decides to keep Quon talking until it does.

"Because you're a fantastic lover. I love to feel you inside me but it is not enough to make me stay."

He runs his hands over his head, pulling his face tight. He tries to grab handfuls of his hair except he does not have enough. So, he rubs the sides of his head furiously with open palms then rushes forward into the closet, scaring the hell out of Jané. She tries reversing even further back but there is nowhere else to go. Quon falls to his knees in front of her. She looks down at him wildly as he wraps his hands around the backs of her thighs.

"Jané, I love you. I will never cheat on you again or hit you. I know I have demons I have to deal with, but putting my hands on you is not one of them. I can be a better man for you. You just have to let me prove it," he wails almost like a child. She hates to see him fall this far this fast. Quon loathes dramatics and does not succumb to them. He has to be hurting genuinely. She just cannot be sure that she will be safe here with Marilyn free or if he will not take her for granted again. She is resigned to taking care of herself first for a change. That means leaving him to deal with whatever his demons are alone.

"I'm sorry, Quon. I really am," she murmurs, wondering if she is in a twisted do over of the night he asked for a divorce. A loud thump echoes through the room before something crashes to the bedroom's floor. The officers appear in the closet's doorway with their guns drawn, finding her huddled in the farthest corner of the closet.

"Mrs. Sullivan, are you okay?" Tanner asks first, oddly. Jané is not okay but she nods anyway and takes a huge gulp of air.

"I'm fine. Quon just—" Her words fail her, her mind deserting her. She feels like she is tumbling in the midst of a hurricane and lost the ability to tell up from down. It does not help that Quon is as confusing as a Rubik's cube and just as confused as she knew he would be after sleeping with him. Now, he has no intentions of letting her go, and it is all her fault for playing with his emotions.

Officer Tanner takes a tiny step forward.

"Mr. Sullivan, put your hands over your head, get up slowly, and walk backwards out of the closet."

Jané watches in a daze as Quon's hands rise over his head. He pushes to his feet. His eyes grow dull as he reverses away.

"I love you, sweetheart. I haven't shown it but I will." Quon's heartfelt avowal nearly buckles Jané's knees, but they are frozen in position. However, she spirals down into a deep sadness, wishing he had not waited until now to say the words she would have given her last breath to hear yesterday, whether he meant them or not. But yesterday is gone and so is her trust in anything he says.

"Jané!" someone yells up the staircase. She knows who it is instantly and fears for his wellbeing. Quon could and probably would go ballistic.

"Stay there, Blazier," she yells back while pushing against the wall to get out of the corner. "I'll come to you!"

Quon growls then stops backing away. Jané backs right back into her corner.

"Keeping coming, Mr. Sullivan," Tanner demands. "Go see who is down there Peterson. I have Mr. Sullivan covered."

Peterson turns and empties the closet doorway. Jané hears when he steps on top of the door and yells, "This is Officer Peterson with Tucson Police Department. Slowly walk to the bottom of the stairs and no further. I am armed and will shoot your ass if you don't obey."

More footsteps assault the door already down.

"I said keep coming, Mr. Sullivan. I will not tell you again." Tanner commands. Quon takes a step back.

"Who are you, sir?" Peterson yells from somewhere in the house.

"I'm Blazier Freeman. I came to get Jané," he responds just as loudly. Quon stops moving backwards and takes a step forward.

"Mr. Sullivan! One more move and you will leave in cuffs for obstruction," Tanner warns then rushes further into the closet, keeping a wide berth between him and Quon. Jané sees her chance to get out, drops the bag on the floor, and runs toward Tanner then behind him.

"Jané," Quon screams. "Dammit, officer, she's leaving me!"

"And she has every right to despite how you feel about it," Tanner responds just as Jané enters the bedroom. "I can't say I blame her after the story you told us in the garage. You are a bad boy, Mr. Sullivan, and you should let her go if you don't want her to find out the rest of your dirty little secrets. No wonder she was swiping at you when we got here. You're lucky she has not performed amateur surgery on your penis," Tanner quips.

Jané wonders how many more secrets one person can possibly have and why he has not told *her* about them, but she is not willing to stick around and find out. She runs towards Peterson standing on the second landing outside the bedroom. He throws up an opened palm. She stops just before stepping on the door.

"Mrs. Sullivan, wait."

"Officer, I know who is downstairs. He came for me."

"Jané," Quon screams, "Don't go with him, baby!"

She ignores him, only wanting her purse and out of this house.

"Can I go, officer?" she asks anxiously.

Peterson frowns.

"I thought you wanted to pack."

"I tried but Quon is acting so strange. I'll get what I need later." Jané does not even want her cell. Quon will call it until she answers and maybe even track her by it. She will not be taking the shit storm that her life has become with her.

Peterson's frown deepens.

"You're sure?"

She nods.

"Just keep Quon here for five minutes. I don't want him to follow me." Jané glances down the stairs at Blazier standing with his hands up like he is a common criminal.

Maybe he did do something wrong when he met me. But I did not know my life would become the equivalent of hell rolled into a series of shit storms when I met him.

Peterson's eyes follow the direction of Jané's pointing downstairs. Then, he motions with his head for her to go. She does not hesitate to move her feet towards Blazier, who starts to grin.

"There is never a dull moment around you, is there, Jané?" he jests. She rushes past him to the kitchen to get her purse off the countertop, except it is not there. She starts to turn in hopeless circles, thinking maybe she carried it into the formal dining room at the back of the kitchen. But she knows she has not been in there in days since dusting all the furniture in the house just to have something to do, and her purse was in plain sight when she retrieved her phone to call Simone.

"Shit! Shit! Shit," she mumbles frantically. "Quon must have hidden it when I went upstairs. Dammit, he is even more desperate to keep me here than I was when the shoe was on the other foot." Jané stops spinning like an aimless leaf blowing in the wind and accepts that she will have to ask Quon what he did with her purse.

She races back to the bottom of the staircase and grasps the knob on the wooden banister, hoping to hold herself together.

"Quon, where is my purse?" she screams at the top of her lungs angrily.

He yells back, "I'll tell you when you tell that fucker to leave!" Blazier snorts, amused by the insult. Jané scowls at him. He only grins harder. More fury swamps her.

"Dammit, Quon, don't act like this! I didn't last night! You have no right to now!"

"I have every right! You're still my wife!"

"Where the hell is it, Quon?" Jané can barely contain herself or believe that her life has spiraled down to childish acts from a man that seems more man than most.

"It's under the sink," he says suddenly. His reply is much quieter than before and reluctant as if he was forced to tell her. She assumes that he probably was, and Tanner had something to do with it, probably offered to jail Quon on some sort of theft charge. At this point, Jané probably would not mind too much if he did. Quon is out of control.

She runs back to the kitchen and realizes along the way why Quon chose the hiding spot that he did. The bottom cabinet doors have no see-through glass. She kneels and tears the doors open, pushes two large pots aside, and finds her purse. She snaps it up and strides quickly for the front door where Blazier already stands talking to Peterson. She looks upstairs. Quon is waiting in the bedroom doorway with Tanner close by his side.

"Jané, don't leave without talking to me first at least," Quon pleads.

"No. I'll call you tomorrow when I come to pick up more of my stuff!" Jané has no intentions of calling for conversational reasons, just to know if he is at work before she comes back to get more of her belongings. If he is not working, she is not coming.

Quon rushes into the hallway. Tanner grabs his arm. Quon spins then careens into Tanner with his shoulder, and drives the cop into the closest wall, face first.

Chapter Nine

Tanner slumps to the floor as Quon races down the stairs toward Jané. Instant paralysis overtakes her body, too shocked that Quon has assaulted a cop to move. Blazier grabs her arm and drags her behind him a second time today. She clenches his shirt in two trembling fists and buries her head in his back.

"Keep your goddamn hands off my wife, Blazier! She is not leaving with you," Quon roars on his way down. Then, flesh strikes flesh. Someone curses. A scuffle ensues. Jané tries to become one with Blazier's body. She is not sure who was struck, does not want to see, but certain that the situation has gone from worst to straight to hell. Then, Blazier's shoulder blades bunch up, hugging her fist like he is raising his hands to ward off something or someone.

"Mr. Sullivan, you need to calm down. Jané is scared to death right now and you're only making it worst," Blazier urges. She is not optimistic that Quon will listen, and expects him to rip her away from the only thing standing between them at any second.

"Baby, look at me," Quon beseeches, his tone beyond desperate now. Jané stays right where she is. She has no idea what he will do next and does not want to see it coming. She has seen too much for one day already.

"Put your hands up, Mr. Sullivan," Peterson shouts suddenly. "You're under arrest for assaulting two police officers."

Two? What the hell did Quon do to Peterson?

"Jané, baby, *look* at me." Quon's demand hangs in the air with lead weighted tension.

"Mr. Sullivan, get down on the ground or we will put you there," Tanner orders.

"I will never hurt you. I'm so sorry, sweetheart." Quon's voice vanishes again. Another scuffle ensues. Blazier jerks against her.

Then, Quon's voice comes back.

"You don't have to go, Jané. I'll leave. Just stay here, baby," he continues to plead. Jané only panics more. He is so determined to keep her here, he assaulted not one, but two cops to make it happen. What will he do to her if she does not stay?

She lets her thoughts go no farther, presses her head even further into Blazier's spine, and tries to remember how to breathe through the terror trying to engulf her. Her life has never been so chaotic, Quon so crazed. Now he is going to jail for the first time since she met him. She really did not want that to happen to him, but Quon should have wanted it to not happen even more.

"Mr. Sullivan, I will not ask you again! Get down or be taken down!" Peterson yells.

Tanner shouts right behind him, "You have two seconds to comply."

Quon follows up with, "Not until Jané looks at me!"

Then, Blazier weighs in on the fiasco, "Just get down, Mr. Sullivan, before they shoot us all!"

Everyone screaming only adds to Jané's emotional crisis and makes her wish that her father was still alive. But he is not and she will have to find the strength to deal with this situation before it goes from hell to somewhere else that none of them can ever come back from.

"Baby, please…just *look* at me!" Quon's pleas seem to come from below her. Since a look is all he seems to want, she glances down at him. He is on his knees again, begging her silently with his eyes as well. She winces when she sees a split in the corner of his bottom lip. If he has an injury, she wonders what the other men look like. She allows her eyes to travel over the officers standing over Quon with both of their guns pointed at his head. Peterson is bleeding from his temple. Tanner will have a fresh black eye from being pushed into the wall in the morning. Jané sets her gaze back on Quon, who does not hesitate to take advantage of her full attention.

"Sweetheart, I'm sorry I'm scaring you. Go with Blazier if it makes you feel better. Just call me tomorrow. Let me know you're okay. Can you do that for me?"

Jané nods like a child and returns his stare. Peterson pushes him face first to the floor then plants his knee in Quon's back. Tanner holsters his gun then reaches behind him and extracts his cuffs before pulling Quon's arms behind him. The cuffs go on. Quon's eyes never leave hers.

"I love you, Jané. Do you hear me?"

She nods again.

"I will never hurt you ever again. Whatever you want, we'll do. Just know that I'll get you—" Quon's words are yanked away when Tanner does the same to his bound wrists to get him off the floor, making Quon grunt in pain. Jané buries her head in Blazier's back again, unable to stand seeing her husband being treated that way even if she is afraid of him. She would have slit her wrists first before believing he would sink this low and hit not one or two, but *three* men today when he has never raised a hand to her.

Well hell, he still hasn't. Just any man he thinks is coming between us. He is even letting me go finally.

Jané begins to question has her Quon ever left but just found the wrongs ways to cope with his world changing. Tanner hauls Quon to his feet and leads him outside the opened front door.

Peterson stays behind.

"Mrs. Sullivan."

"Yeah," Jané says into the wall of muscles in front of her, not certain if the cop understands her since her words are muffled. Nor does she care.

"Are you okay?"

"No," she admits pitifully.

Peterson sighs.

"Mr. Sullivan will probably be out by morning. Whatever you're taking from here I advise you to get it now and be someplace else when your husband gets home."

"He won't hurt me…though any man in the area is at risk."

Blazier sniggers.

"She's right. He sucker punched me earlier today too. I'm inclined to believe he actually loves her."

Peterson snorts.

"She does seem to bring out the worst in him, that's for sure. I came to make a vandalism report and caught his wedding ring to the forehead."

Blaze releases a deep laugh from his chest.

"He does pack quite a punch."

"That he does," Peterson confesses unenthusiastically. "Okay, Mrs. Sullivan, I'm leaving and giving my card to Blazier. If anything else happens call me. I also wrote the number down for the wrecker that I called for your car who will take it to a mechanic in the morning at ten. I'll try to hold Mr. Sullivan as long as I can. Have a good night you two...*if* you can.

Jané feels Blazier's torso shift to one side like he is reaching for something in his pocket. She shifts with it until he straightens up.

"Thank you, Peterson. Jané is coming with me. If you need to reach her, call this number."

She senses when the officer's presence wane, hears when his cruiser quietly leaves her driveway. Still, she stands with her head and fists submerged in Blazier's shirt with her eyes closed, doing her best to hide from the world.

"Jané," Blazier calls softly.

"Hmmm," she answers even quieter.

"We need to lock up and leave, sweetheart."

But, Jané has already left mentally. It would be pure hell on her mind to come back, so it does not. Her fingers work by themselves to unclench before her head unearths itself. Her feet step back. When she misses the warmth and protection of Blazier instantly, only then does her mind willingly return to the rest of her body. She shakes her head.

I am already depending on a man that I just met. This is so not fucking good but that seems to be the theme for this day that just will not end.

Jané's world as she knew it is completely gone. She is not sure what to do with this one. The new one she thought she would have is impossible as long as Marilyn is free and Quon is acting manic.

Blazier turns around and peers down at her. She glances up and receives an unhealthy serving of compassion from his eyes.

More fucking pity.

Jané never wanted to be subjected to that again, except it is happening and she loses the little composure that she had.

Her chin wobbles, vision grows cloudy right after. She hates immediately that she cannot stop her own emotions from consuming her in front of Blazier, who steps forward and wraps his arms around her. Her tiny body vanishes in his embrace then he starts to rock her gently.

"It's okay, Jané. You've been through a lot in only a day and you need to let it out." She could not have kept it inside anyway. It is already escaping so she lets the turbulent feelings empty themselves into his chest. However, she is determined this will be her last cry. So, her mind begins to hurry through each event that brought Quon and her to this point as if it is searching for any and every moment that held some emotional block she had put up, and broke it down. It does not take long for Jané to fall completely apart in Blazier's arms.

She cries for her failed marriage that won't stop failing, her ruined car that she does not know when she can replace. Even Quon's arrest and the secrets that he kept and is still keeping, find a way into her sorrow. Her mind stops flipping through painful moments in time to let her question how Quon managed to keep so many secrets inside and run a successful company while living a lie with her, and maintaining a mistress.

No wonder he wanted a divorce. He had too much on his plate and something had to go. I would bet Blazier's whole body that it was easier for Quon to let me go since I know the least about the real him.

Jané may not know as much as she thought about Quon, but she is dead certain he wanted to keep his double life and her from looking at him as anything other than the man she loves. No one wants to look bad in anyone's eyes. What she does not get is why Quon could not let go after she gave him a part of the real her that she keeps hidden. She only wanted to say goodbye and give him something to remember her by after her world fell apart. Instead, everything came crashing down around him, too. The very thing he would have wanted to prevent. Maybe one day she will tell him how freeing it is to just be yourself.

The well of tears finally runs dry. Jané has no concept of time, only aware of Blazier rocking her. She grasps his bulky body even tighter to her. He is becoming the only anchor that she has left in Arizona. She thought Simone was one. Someone who cares for her and would keep their promises, like calling or coming by when Jané did not show up for their date. When Jané adds up all of Simone's strange behavior that started at Sensual's, she realizes she does not know her best friend anymore either. Simone should have been here long before now. But, Jané has more pressing problems that require her attention much more than Simone's odd personality that keeps getting odder.

She rubs her face into Blazier's chest.

God, his chest is so wide. And if I don't let him go, I won't be able to.

She lifts eyes that have been ravaged by an ugly cry, to Blazier's. She knows they are red and swollen, but it does not faze her for him to see her at her worst. He met her at her worst, and now he grins down at her.

"Okay now?"

She nods, and it is true for once.

"But I can't guarantee I won't go cry baby again on you though," she quips to lighten the somber mood that seems to be permanently attached to the house now.

"That's fine. If you're crying, you're feeling, and working your way past all this. Now let's lock up, pack some things for you, and go before your car bandit comes back. I like my truck just the way it is," he jests, getting only a small smile from her.

She wastes no time going around him to the kitchen to check both garage accesses that are open. Blazier trails her into the garage where she retrieves Quon's remote for his car, or risk cutting herself to get hers. The Mercedes' seats are filled with glass that did not find its way to the ground. When both doors to the house are locked tight, they check other points of entry to make sure those are too. Jané ignores how much better she feels with Blazier here, just as good as she would feel if Quon was. They finally make it upstairs and have to pass a jagged spot in wall before going into the bedroom.

Damn Quon. Why did you have to sink us this low?

Jané shakes her head and walks inside the bedroom, and then the closet where the duffel bag lays abandoned on the floor. She picks it up and discovers her phone lying underneath it. She must have dropped them both when Quon changed disturbingly for the umpteenth time today. Simone still has not reached out to Jané, who lets the bizarre behavior from the people she loves bother her for a split second more before tapping out a short message to her friend. Jané lets her know that Quon has been arrested, her car vandalized, and she is going somewhere safe for the night. Then, she drops the cell phone on the nightstand and rushes to her dresser by the window.

Blazier sits down on the bed to wait and watch patiently for her to grab underwear. When she has a handful, a massive load of guilt for putting him through so much when he has not known her a New York minute settles in her chest. She turns around to face him.

"Look, I'm—" He shakes his head before she can say more.

"Jané, don't apologize or tell me to go without you. I'm not leaving and you're not making me do anything I don't want to. Accept my help because it's here to stay."

She does not think it is possible to feel any guiltier than she already is, but she does after he makes a vow to be the friend that Simone is not right now.

"But, Blazier, I don't have anywhere to go and you can't drive me around all night until I can find a replacement for my car."

"You can stay with me. I promise you a perfectly clean guest bedroom with an attached bathroom and both have locks."

Damn, what does he really move? Weight? Kilos? Get out of your head, Jané. That is none of your business. But going home with him is. There is no telling what you will try to do to the man, or with him.

Images of his body over hers, or under, attack her mind. She pushes them away but not fast enough to keep a small inferno from igniting in her core.

"You can take me to a hotel. I'll be fine there," she suggests breathlessly.

"But *I* won't be, Jané. Not when you have people destroying a perfectly good car with the owner nearby. That's not your common criminal. I'd feel better with you close by where they'll have to go through me to get to you. The cops know where you are. So you will be perfectly safe too."

But will you be safe, Blazier?

Jané begins to giggle quietly at her own scandalous thoughts.

"I'm starting to think you like standing between me and my problems," she jokes.

"I do," he whispers, bringing her humor to a crashing halt. Shock takes over.

"Why?" she asks softly.

"Because you need it and I like you."

Jané's head reels when the chance arrives to find out just how much he likes her. It takes her several seconds to act on it, and she has to swallow first to wet her throat, suddenly gone dry.

"Like me how?" she asks hoarsely, nervously. His hands run down his powerful thighs cased in dark jeans. His behind lifts from the bed, bringing him to his feet that turn toward her and starts to carry him to her.

"Just like your husband said. I want to sleep with you. I was attracted to you from our phone conversation without ever laying eyes on you. It's why I came personally to move your furniture when I didn't have to. But I know a woman like you who is use to things like this would not want someone like me."

Jané is taken aback. Blazier just called her snob to her face. It irritates her that he judges books by their covers, too.

"I did not buy any of this, Blazier. The only thing that bears my name is wrecked. Every penny I spend belongs to Quon. I have nothing. So what would a man like you, who are not just a mover obviously, want with a woman like me, destitute and soon to be starving?" she asks snippily.

He stops in front of her. His hands rise slowly to push the drape of her hair back from her face before framing it with his long fingers. Mini electrical storms discharge on her cheeks. He stares into Jané's eyes until she thinks he will kiss her. She waits for it to happen, knowing that it should not, wanting it to all same. Then, he says, "Everything."

She was not expecting that answer and is taken completely off guard.

"Everything," she mimics in a hushed tone. But, she cannot handle everything with another man, not now, maybe not ever. At least, she thinks she cannot. But Blazier makes her want to try. Then, he nods. His head dips. Suddenly, his lips are on hers. Razor-sharp sensations spiral through her body and take her breath away. She opens her mouth to breathe. His tongue slips inside, glides across hers, and makes her senses scatter. She moans and twists her head to the side so he has better access to her mouth. His hands fall away. He steps back. The little bolts streaking down her face stop, so does the heat from his hand warming her from the outside in. She is left drowning in her own reactions to his kiss. He stares at her as if he is waiting for her to collect herself. It takes a moment, but she finally opens her eyes and straightens up.

He smiles down on her.

"I want everything, Jané, but you aren't ready for *anything*. You've gone through too much and I suspect there is a lot more coming your way before things get better for you. And yes I'll be your shield and only that until you're ready for everything. Now finishing packing, so we can go," he orders softly. Her hand completes the toss of the underwear into the bag haphazardly. He could have yelled and not have gotten a faster reaction from her. Her feet move to the bathroom to grab the bare bones of beauty products that she drops into her shoes on top of clothes in the bag. On her way out, she zips it up.

He takes it from her and asks, "Do you want your phone?"

She shakes her head, not sure if Simone will respond to the text she sent. Jané hopes her best friend is not in some kind of trouble, too, and unable to let her know. Blazier takes the lead down the stairs then stands by with his hand in the small of her back as she sets the alarm. She finds it difficult to remember the pin number with her body reheating under his touch. When her mind finally coughs up the numbers to her parents' anniversary, she enters them quickly. They exit the house. Jané is surprised to find a personal black truck with huge four doors and extended cab parked on the street. She assumed he would be picking her up in a less glamorous truck or even the one he drove here earlier, and she would have been glad to climb in either one if it got her the hell away from here.

Nope, he does not move just damn furniture.

Blazier takes her elbow and leads her to his vehicle then has to help her in. When she is seated then belted, he pitches her bag in the backseat and climbs in the driver's. He cranks the diesel monster and rolls away from the only home Jané has known for four years. It is strange for her to be sleeping somewhere else tonight, with someone she just met, all because Blazier deems himself her savior just when she needs one, or two.

Someone may have to save me from my damn self when it comes to Blazier and Quon.

Jané has no illusions that Quon can still set her body on fire, but so does Blazier.

And I can't have them both at the same time. Or can I? I think you just went too far, Jané, now stop damn thinking.

She obeys her own command. The ride becomes quiet. Fortunately it is short, so the atmosphere does not have time to get uncomfortable. They drive up to a wrought iron gate that stands at least eight feet tall. Jané considers asking Blazier has he forgotten where he lives. Then, the gate opens and he drives through. A smooth-stoned gray mansion with three-levels comes into view, confusing her becomes.

"Blazier, who lives here?"

"I do," he states plainly, too plainly for her.

"But you work for a moving company," she hurls back warily.

"Sometimes I do."

Now, she is frustrated with his broad answers, and cannot understand why he chooses to keep so much of his life covert when he knows so much about hers.

"Then what do you do when you're not working for the moving company? I'm not being nosy on purpose. I'm just not interested in squatting in someone else's home," she explains as they follow a straightaway to the front of the house with a half-moon staircase that would eclipse the front of her home. Blazier parks and cuts off the engine while she peers into several lit windows beside her.

"I own the company when I'm not just working for it," he says suddenly.

Jané takes a hit from the blind side. Her eyes swerve to his.

"You wanted me to think you were just a working stiff, didn't you?"

He nods.

"I'm not Ray Charles. I don't like gold diggers."

"I could still try and use you for your money, you know. I am penniless, homeless, car less, phone less," she banters though it is the absolute truth.

He starts to laugh wildly.

"You choose to be all those things, Jané, but we both know Quon won't let you go without even if you wanted him to. *I* most certainly won't let you live that way even though you're not mine. And if you were a gold digger, you would not be trying to leave your husband."

"Yeah that's true, but it doesn't mean I wouldn't try to use you for your money."

"If that was the case, you wouldn't even suggest it. You'd already be in my lap telling me what you wanted."

"Got a lot of experience with gold diggers, huh," she mocks.

Blazier opens his door, turns to get out of it, and looks back, "Too much."

Jané undoes her seatbelt and grabs for the handle of her door.

"Sit, Jané." he says suddenly.

She hesitates then puts her hand back in her lap, waiting for him to circle the truck. He opens her door and encircles her waist with both hands. Hers find his thick forearms lightly coated with springy hair that tickles her palms. When she cannot get her fingers all the way around his upper arms, she likes it. She likes that her hands cannot close around Quon's forearms too, so maybe she should not be so thrilled about it. But, she is anyway.

"Jesus, what do you lift...*cars*?"

Blaze chuckles before setting her on her feet but his hands stay put.

"No. I got these guns from lifting boxes before I took over my grandfather's companies across the state." Jané frowns then does a double take when he mentions *companies*, letting more information about himself slip out.

She squints up at him.

"Blazier, you do realize I'm not going to ask you for anything or steal from you. It's okay to tell me things. I'll keep your secrets." Then she realizes that she desires his trust like he has hers.

She has no earthly idea when she gave it to him but they can hardly be friends if he has no faith in her, too.

He peers down at her, maybe looking for hard evidence that she will not betray him. She guesses he does not trust easily after his divorce. Maybe he even has secrets like Quon that he needs to keep hidden, too. She decides to take him off the hot seat. It is too early in their relationship to demand a come to Jesus meeting anyway.

She taps his arms with nerveless fingers.

"Listen. Forget about it. Let's go inside."

He nods then drops his hands to reach behind her and get her bag out of the backseat. He turns and leads the way up his front steps doubling as a stairway to heaven. They are just that long, with double wide oak doors at the end that stand almost as tall as the gates circling the property.

Jané enters a round foyer that could house her home comfortably, but only holds one lonely round table with the biggest bouquet of flowers she has ever seen. She starts to spin slowly while taking in the nothingness under a dome ceiling with a skylight above. A chandelier appears to be dropping down out of it. She suspects the architect likes anything to do with circles.

"What is it with you people and your space?" she asks condescendingly. She does not like the monstrosity of a home at all. It seems a lonesome place to be with probably thousands of square feet between you and the next breather. Jané would rather be close in every way to those she loves.

She comes to a standstill finally in front of Blazier, who is watching her too closely for her skin to not prickle under his probing gaze. It is as if he is waiting for her reaction to the great hall. She shakes her head and giggles quietly.

He frowns.

"Was that a racist question?"

Jané snickers, not offended by his concern for reverse racism.

"It probably was racist. Why? Did I hurt your feelings? You can take me home if you like. I don't mind." Actually, she does mind. She is not looking forward to being home alone in either house. But, her home puts her close to other warm bodies that can give her sense of security if something happens. Her neighbors are only a hedge bush away and nice for the most part. Blazier will probably sleep a floor away and Jané does not want to be alone right now. She has six months of that under her belt already.

He shakes his head and swipes at her arm softly.

"I upset you. I'm sorry."

"Actually I thought I upset you, but I'd rather be alone at home. Your house is too big. Sorry," she adds sheepishly. He begins to laugh until it fills up the foyer. Jané did not think that was possible as big as it is, but Blazier's hilarity has no problem doing it.

Then, he spreads his arms wide.

"Are you serious? You'd rather be somewhere else than here?" he asks with shock mingling with his mirth. She simply nods.

"Why?" he asks, as his eyes grow wide. Jané hugs herself and rubs her elbows like she is cold. In a way, she is.

"I don't feel secure here and you don't seem all that comfortable with me invading your *personal* space," she says flippantly then scans the wide open area again, contemplating who needs miles of personal space, unless they have something to hide.

His laughter dies a quick death. Then he scans the room.

"It's not that I'm uncomfortable. I hate being alone but it's hard to know who to trust when just about everyone wants *this*."

"Well, you can count me out of that clique. I already know you don't trust me and I rather not be here," she admits, distracted by the high ceiling too far up to provide adequate lighting, making creepy shadowy spots in the rounded corners of the foyer. No home is supposed to feel this forlorn or chilling.

Blaze frowns.

"You're serious, aren't you?"

She gives him a grave glance.

"*Dead* serious. I'll meet you at the truck." She pivots to go back the way she came when a hand seizes her upper arm, halting anymore steps forward. She sways back around to Blazier, who is studying her like an insect under a microscope.

"Don't go, Jané," he murmurs.

Immediately she feels a kindred spirit in him; someone who does not want to be alone ever, would be alright if they are, but hates it all the same.

"Okay," exits her mouth before she thinks about it. He is as desperate for company as she. She cannot in good conscience leave him alone after all that he has done for her today.

His shoulders sag like he has just taken on the weight of the world. Or maybe he was afraid she would say no. Jané wants to know which one is the truth. He does not trust her but it is like he needs her to stay. She decides to not push the issue when she becomes too exhausted to stand here any longer.

"Can I ask a favor, Jané?" he asks out of nowhere after a heavy silence falls around them.

"Yeah," she says cagily, unsure of what he could possibly want from her. She has nothing to give.

"Sleep with me," he says suddenly and takes her by surprise.

Chapter Ten

She flinches and shrieks, "What! No!" But she is in no way disgusted by his request or going to admit that it holds a lot more appeal than it should for her.

Blaze snorts.

"Not for sex, Jané. In the same bed, yes. I know you're married." His tone lowers to sternly sober, his eyes intensify. "I respect that, as much as I may not want to and you're not ready for me."

Jané would like to know why he keeps saying that she is not ready for him. She does not ask however. With questions come answers and actions she may not be able to resist carrying out in her weakened state of mine. Quon has broken her. Marilyn has tried to frighten her. Her world is adrift. Blazier will be cemented as the replacement anchor that she needs so badly. She cannot risk that with her unhealthy attachment issues. She thinks she should tell him that is she no walk in the park.

She places a hand on his forearm, gripping it tightly.

"Blazier, I need to be honest with you. I think you're one of the most beautiful men I've met next to Quon. But since my parents died, I've looked for the love and support they gave me in other people. Quon gave me that for a time and I attached to him enough that his life became mine. When he took that away, it nearly killed me inside."

Blaze grips her outstretched arm with his empty hand.

"And then you walked away, Jané."

Her mouth falls open in shock at her actions. She never considered that she did let go without much of a fight.

"You don't attach unhealthily, Jané, or you would have held on to your husband for dear life no matter what he did to you. You loved him unconditionally like most women do and there is nothing wrong with that. You're supposed to form attachments to loved ones. Quon is the one having trouble letting go."

Jané always thought *she* is the one that holds on too tightly and maybe unintentionally pushed Quon away. Now she thinks maybe his secrets did the job for her. She used what little strength she had left to give him what he wanted.

"I loved him enough to let him go," she whispers.

Blazier nods.

"That's healthy. Now attach to me and keep me company tonight. And I'll do the same for you."

Jané hears him and murmurs, "Okay," but she is living inside her head at the moment, wondering if she got her marriage all wrong with Quon from the start. She is not too happy about Quon filling her head either.

Damn I have the man at the brain and all he has done lately is hurt me. How the hell do I stop loving him?

The answer never comes to Jané as she follows Blazier blindly out the other end of the foyer to a double staircase that seems a mile long. On the second level, they take enough twists and turns to convince her she will never find the first floor again. Then, her stomach grumbles. Blazier chuckles. She gives him a shy smile until they reach a bedroom so big it has enough furniture to outfit a whole apartment where her mouth drops open.

Couches and chaise lounges with a full set of tables, sit in front of opened balcony doors letting the night breeze play with the sheer curtains pulled aside. A theater-sized television the same width and length as her entertainment center at home, takes up the wall at the foot of an enormous bed that makes a California king look like a twin. The room is a supersized man cave decked out in black and brown with huge potted plants reaching for the ceiling. Jané likes this room way better than she does the foyer.

Blaze points to a door to the right of them.

"The bathroom's that way. I'll go get us something to eat. The remote for the TV is on the nightstand. Make yourself at home."

"That is not even possible," she says flippantly, while scanning a leather headboard mounted to the wall and stretching several feet out pass the bed.

"All the more reasons to make sure you know you are welcomed to. I'll be back in five."

"Make it three or I'm coming to find you," she warns, distracted by the expanse of the black and brown bed set. She is afraid if he threw the covers back on her, she could get lost in the shiny, thick material with diamonds woven through it.

"Don't or it'll take me a day to find you," he jests. Jané whirls her head around like she is possessed, praying he is joking. But, he looks serious.

"You're not kidding are you?" she asks dryly.

He shakes his head.

"We're at the back of the house. It will take you a month to learn the layout so stay here. There's an intercom by the door. Press 2 for the kitchen. I'll pick up."

He walks out and shuts the door behind him. It gets eerily quiet. Jané feels like she is cut off from the rest of the world and moves to the table doubling as a nightstand. On it is a black lamppost pretending to be a lamp. She pinches the remote from under it, wanting the TV on for background noise. Then, she kicks her shoes off, gets on the bed between two fireplaces on each side and constructed from the same stones as the house.

It would probably take two fireplaces to heat this room and take all day and night to do it.

She folds her lean body into an Indian style position in the middle of the bed covers, before bringing the big screen to life and begins to play mad flipper with the remote. She has surfed through hundreds of channels when Blazier returns with a tray burdened with everything from the food chart, cups of wine, and bottles of chilled water. She suspects he will gobble down two thirds of it himself. It is fine with her. She is not a big eater anymore since she stopped the birth control.

Blaze sets the tray down on the bed then pushes it to Jané's side before he follows it. When he kneels like a praying God beside her, she has a hard time selecting what to eat first.

Everything looks so damn good. He is going to spoil me. Now why the hell am I complaining?

"Eat, Jané," he commands with a stern stare then pulls his white polo shirt over his head, exposing her to his washboard abs and pectorals that seem bigger than her breasts. Her eyes trace tribal tattoos at the tops of his upper arms. Her stare starts to border on rude. Then, he tosses his shirt to the floor.

Fuck! He is gorgeous everywhere and in so much trouble with me here.

Blazier returns her stare that has become downright ogling.

"Sorry. I don't associate the bed with clothes. If you're uncomfortable, I can put my shirt back on." His voice snaps her out of a daze.

"Don't be uncomfortable in your own bed," she says huskily.

"For you, I would be fine with it," he says somberly.

She grins.

"I'm fine with it. You're just.... umm—" She almost says exactly what is on her mind and thinks better of it. Informing him of how sexy he is shirtless will push things to a whole other level between them. They have not cleared the first one of simply getting to know each other yet.

He cocks his head.

"What?"

"Nothing," she chirps quickly then stuffs her mouth with a strawberry. Blazier continues to stare at her curiously. Eventually, he twists his mouth in defeat and sinks his backside into the bed. She sighs in relief, glad that he left it alone and pops another piece of fruit into her mouth while changing the channels on the television. She settles on an action film and drops the remote between them.

He glances down at it then at the side of Jané's face until it starts to burn under his stare.

"You can watch a chick flick. I don't mind."

"And have another reason to cry again? I don't think so," she retorts, slightly horrified he has already seen her cry twice in one day when they have not known each other but hours. Yet, she is in his home and has been given the privileges of a girlfriend.

Talk about moving fast and he doesn't even trust me.

Jané starts to become uneasy after that thought. How were they going to be friends if he cannot talk about himself with her?

She guesses they will not after all, and it saddens her.

"What is it, Jané?" he asks. She realizes she is frowning.

"I just wondered how we were going to be good friends if you can't talk to me."

He blows a puff of air, cooling off her flesh heating under his eyes before he begins to peer even harder at her. Then, he turns his back suddenly, and waits for her to notice a tattoo on his left shoulder blade in the form of a swastika.

The fruit in Jané's hand clatters to the platter as her blood in her fingers run cold, making them useless. The feeling quickly invades the rest of her body.

"*Holy hell*," she shrieks but cannot think of what to do next nor move if she could.

Blazier shifts back around then looks at her regretfully and smirks.

"One of the bad roads I traveled down."

"Why?" she whispers, scared clean out of her good sense or she would have made a break for the door.

Why did he bring me here if he hates blacks and probably other races too? Revenge? To atone for some sin? Oh God, please don't let it be because he still pities me.

That would be the worse reason out of all of the ones scrambling around her head.

"Jané," he calls softly.

"What?" She has to force the word out of her mouth, convinced that she has just been deceived into thinking someone cared for her, again.

"I'm not a bigot," he murmurs. She is no hurry to believe him.

"Says the man with the hate symbol on his back," she snaps, suddenly angry.

"Can I tell you why it's there?" The pleading in his baritone is unmistakable and weaves through her fury to the heart of it, her heart.

"Tell me, and then you can take me home."

"I don't think you'll leave me when I tell you why. I think you'll understand but you can't prejudge me."

Jané raises a knee to prop her arm up then glares at him.

"Try me." Her tone is hard but she wants to know the story then leave still.

I will probably always want to know what his story is...Where the hell did that thought come from?

Yet, it is too late to take the thought back or undo the attraction between them that created it. She is stuck with loving one man, possibly falling head over heels for another, and rather not think about any of it.

Blazier scoots closer.

"My wife, Pamela, cheated on me with a black man about five years ago. They're still together and I go to the house every once in a while now. But in the beginning, I hated them both for ruining my life. So I joined a hate group called White Devils. I needed an outlet for the pain of losing her to him but I didn't nor have I ever hated your whole race, just him. But when you're two sheets to the wind every waking hour, good judgment goes out the window. After my mother got wind of who my new friends were, she called Pamela, who found me at the clubhouse one morning passed out in some groupie's bed. Greg, Pamela's lover at the time, now husband, drove her there. Who does that?" Blazier frowns. Jané giggles then quiets to listening.

"Anyway, they waited for me to get up then convinced me to go to a private rehab. What made me decide to go was when Pamela offered to get back with me in front of Greg if it would set me back on the right path. He approved it. He told me that he knew he'd destroyed my life but he would step back if it would fix it. At the rehab center is where I realized that in the wrong state of mind, I allowed my body to be permanently stained with hate, Pamela's betrayal, and someone else's belief." He stops talking abruptly. Jané is not convinced that he has told her the whole story.

"What happened next?" she asks when he seems like he will not continue.

He grins, knowing he had her.

"Nothing. I refused to take Pamela back. I don't trust her, remember, but I also loved her enough to let her go. I recognized Greg had set her on the right path as well. She liked cocaine. So did me and the brotherhood. But Pamela and I threw many wild parties here centered around our drug of choice before I met them. And trust me when I tell you that not everybody dislikes this house like you," he quips then begins to play with Jané's fingers dangling over her knee. They become fascinating to him.

"But our lifestyle was killing Pamela. Greg saved her after they started an affair on her computer analyst job...And then they saved me."

Jané forgets to be angry since his story has a happy ending and not the components to make her run screaming into the night. But she has not forgotten about the tattoo.

"Why keep the swastika then? Cause I have to tell you it doesn't make a great impression to someone of my race or probably any race other than yours."

"To remind myself of my mistakes," he states plainly.

"Ah, Blazier, it's *behind* you," she counters smartly then makes the connection for his reason for keeping the terrible mark.

He nods.

"Correct. In the past but not forgotten so I won't repeat it."

Jané squints until she can only see his eyes, and does not know what to make of him. He does not trust easily and has a hate symbol on his body. But he forgave a man who stole something precious from him, and allowed the man to save him. Then, he paid it forward and rescued her twice in one day. Now, he trusts her with one of the most disturbing but defining moments in his life, a story of redemption if Jané ever heard one.

"Well what happens now?" he mutters. She feels the overwhelming need to touch him, and dives across the bed to wrap her arms around his neck. She understands what it took to tell his past, spilling his darkest secrets to someone that could have condemned him for his actions. Opening herself up for rejection is not something Jané thrives on either, and no one should ever be punished for doing it.

"I'll stay," she murmurs into his neck.

He groans.

"Why did you have to touch me?" He asks huskily before his arms encircle her waist and falls forward. Jané lands on her back under him, giving her a sense of security that has been long gone. Then, his mouth drops down on hers, making her senses reel into the night sky. When his tongue spears her lips seeking an entrance, she opens and moans from the contact setting her body ablaze within.

She wants him as much as she does Quon, who explodes through her mind again. She pushes his image away. She does not owe him anything anymore although her vows still mean something to her. She wants to keep them sacred for as long as she can. But she has no idea how long she can hold out before giving herself to Blazier, who grinds his erection into her thigh. She gets the immediate feeling that he is every bit as well-endowed as she thought he was, and forgets to hold on to her vows.

Her legs spread wide and grow super soaked at the center of them. Her senses engulf the mahogany scent attached to his skin so different from Quon's Aspen. She remembers unwillingly that he is not Quon, nor is Quon here, and she should not be either. So she begins to wind the kiss down before they go too far, moving her tongue around Blazier's slower and slower until he withdraws then lifts his head. He untangles an arm from beneath her and runs his thumb over her lips.

"You're not ready, are you?" he whispers with his eyes glued to her mouth.

She smiles again the pad of his finger.

"More ready than you know but it is not the right time."

"You're still married," he deadpans. She nods. He smiles. Jané hopes it is a sign of respect and he does not think she is a tease. He rolls off her then the bed and stands up with a small smile still playing on his face.

"I'm going to put on some pajamas. What do you want me to pull out of your bag for you?"

She searches her mind then groans and covers her face.

"I didn't pack any nightclothes."

"I have a shirt you can sleep in," he offers.

"That's fine." She sits up and watches him move like a silent predator across the plush tan carpet to a dresser twice as big as hers. In a middle drawer, he extracts a set of neatly folded pajamas. He walks back to her and gives her the top.

"Thanks," she murmurs. He grins again and strolls toward the bathroom with the bottoms. It seems so intimate for them to wear a matching set of nightwear to bed, something Jané has never done with Quon. She did not know such a small gesture can make her feel so close to someone. It is a good thing she and Quon are divorcing soon or their marriage would be in a bigger pile of trouble than it already is. She is playing with fire being in close proximity to Blazier when she desires him completely. The bathroom door closes behind him. She scrambles to the edge of the bed to undress hurriedly and redress in the button down silk shirt with long sleeves.

Considering the shirt is three sizes too big, she feels decent. Mentally, she cannot claim the privilege. Nor will the shirt be a sufficient barrier if Blazier starts a fire that only letting him inside her will extinguish. Jané vows to keep her wits about her and her hands to herself if she does not want to be like Quon, a cheater.

She crawls back across the bed, after stuffing her clothes into her bag sitting on a black velvet chaise near the balcony doors. When she resumes her seat in the middle of the coverlet, Blazier is standing in the opened doorway frozen. She glances at him before picking up the remote and throwing a cracker topped with cheddar cheese into her mouth.

"What's wrong?" she asks much more nonchalantly than she feels. Her center began to pulse as soon as she saw him watching her.

"I'm keeping my distance until I cool off," he says hoarsely, strangely.

Jané trains a worried glance on him, with every intention of looking him in the face, but her eyes get no higher than his chest.

"Why, are you hot?" She hopes she can appear to be concerned about him and not get caught staring rudely at his body, but she does not hold out much hope.

He coughs.

"You were crawling across the bed when I came out. It…affected me," he explains, and does not need to go into more details for her.

"Sorry," she says softly, knowing they are in an even bigger shit storm than her marriage is turning out to be.

"Don't be," he utters in a deep timbre that bathes her skin in heat.

"Jané, I just…liked it too much. Now give me a few minutes." He pivots around then slams the door closed.

She puts her eyes back on the television with a faint smile.

At least I'm not the only one suffering.

The shower comes on and pulls her eyes right back toward the bathroom. Jané is no idiot. She knows exactly what he is about to do, or already doing. A spicy thought to join him crosses her mind, but she is tired. The food has settled in her stomach and made her more than relaxed. She suspects Blazier's company has a lot to do with that as well but does not zoom in on the thought or risk giving her desire more fuel and room for her fantasies to grow.

Instead, she decides sleep is the better choice and a lot easier on Blazier if she is covered from head to toe and not affecting him when he leaves the bathroom. The thick mattress under her is begging to be stretched out on. She lifts the platter to the nightstand then pulls the cover back and slips under it. As soon as her head hits one of several cushiony pillows, she yawns. Blazier is not even in the room and yet she feels protected. But he is the reason, and one day she will pay it forward. For now, she will sleep.

It is not long after Jané closes her eyes, a hand lightly stroking the back of her head pulls her from a deep sleep. This is not the first time she has felt it either. The touch would wake her then lull her back to oblivion. She finally rolls over to a wide awake Blazier, who is supporting his head with his knuckles. His elbow pierces the bed as he lies on his side in the dark only broken up by moonlight filtering through the glass doors.

"Why aren't you sleeping?" she asks groggily.

"I can't," he says casually then lifts a hand to the side of her head and strokes her hair again.

"Need me to go in another room?" she offers out of sheer courteous because she does not want to sleep anywhere else alone.

His hand leaves her hair, spreads in the middle of her back, and slides her face first into his chest.

"Absolutely not. I'll get over my fascination with you in a little bit, hopefully. Now go back to sleep." But, she cannot. She wants him so she stares at him. He groans before his head drops, and his tongue skims her lips. She opens her mouth and lets her palate trace his lips. He groans again before shifting his body over hers. She lets her legs fall apart to give him room between him. His hand pushes under her shirt then glides up her thigh. Her ability to think fractures as her chest swells with desire too big for her body. It compresses her lungs, making it impossible for her to breathe. Time stands still when his hand cups the mound between her legs as his tongue dances on her.

Moisture seeps from her core, allowing him to slip a finger inside her. She pants against his mouth, and lifts her leg so he can have more room to do whatever he wants with her. She knew she would let him if he ever got this close, and should be regretting it. Instead, she closes her eyes to enjoy it his fingers that seem to be everywhere, thrusting in and out of her inner walls and doing slow paces around the tiny bundle of nerves hidden in the apex of her thighs. A sleeping orgasm stirs and sends jolts of sensation through her center, making her walls clench around his fingers.

Blazier grins against her mouth.

"So soon, Jané? I need to teach you how to wait."

She could not wait if someone offered her all the money in the world.

"The time to teach is not now, Blazier. I'm almost there," she groans.

"I know and I'll give you what you want this time, sweetheart, but you will work for it next time," he warns. She wishes she could deny that there will be a next time between them. But, she likes his hand on her, making her mind spin as surges of bliss crash against the walls his fingers inhabit, and pushing her over the edge. However, the only thing she intends on putting in work for is surviving the waves of cum rushing through her channel while his fingers drive in and out of the ripples, making them last longer than normal.

She bites her bottom lip to keep from yelling out. Her back arches, trying to bear the brunt of the storm raging inside of her. When it passes, Blazier removes his hand by trailing his finger across her swollen clit. Pulses ripple through her. She shudders. He grins then drops both of his elbows beside her head. Her back finds the mattress again. She pants until her body cools down, and then remembers that Blazier did not cum, too. But, he does not seem all that concerned about being not getting his turn while watching her return to normal below him.

She rolls her head sideways on the pillow.

"What about you, Blazier?"

"That was about you, Jane. You needed a good note to end this day on, but you're still not ready for me."

Something tells her to not ask him why he keep saying that she is not ready for him. She might not like the answer, or love it too much. He shifts his body to the side of her and resumes the same position she found him in when she woke up. She rolls to her side, cuddles in his chest, and closes her eyes. Yet, she feels his watching her, over her, making her feel just as safe before Quon blew her world apart.

Another caress of Blazier's hand in her hair creates the same lulling sensation that woke her. Now, it entices her to drift off without a second thought about the stranger next to her quickly becoming what Quon is no longer, her refuge in a world that she does not recognize.

When she wakes again, the room is brightly lit with natural light pouring in from the balcony. She hears feet pounding the marble floor in the hallway outside the closed bedroom door. She is in the same position she went to sleep in on the last stroke of Blazier's hand. She has not felt this rested in months.

"Jané," he yells before crashing into the room. She sits up and grins drowsily.

"Yes." She takes in his snug jeans outlining his manhood that bulges even when he is not hard before making her eyes travel up his body to the black teé framing his torso like a lover. Her mouth waters. He rushes the bed with a worried look that begins to worry her.

"You need to get up, sweetheart. There's trouble at your house again."

Oh no, no, no! So this is how it feels to repeat the same fucking day over and over.

Jané gets a gut churning feeling that she will not enjoy this do over either, but still has to face it.

She plants a hand on Blazier's pillow and pushes herself to the edge of the bed.

"What happened?" she asks frantically as he crosses the room and snatches her bag from its seat in the sun on his chair. He hauls it to her and drops it on the bed. She jumps to her feet and begins to shift through the contents, while speculating about what could be going wrong at her home this time. She slings the first pieces of clean clothing that her hand touches on the bed.

Blazier starts to back away in her side vision.

"Your neighbors called the cops about ten minutes ago when the alarm went off. They knew the house was empty from last night's *festivities*."

"But nobody saw what happened?" she asks then reaches for the buttons on Blazier's shirt.

"No, but apparently, several of your neighbors reported a hole in your living room's window, the husband in jail, and the wife gone. A guard told Quon what was happening. He asks the guard to get in touch with Peterson, who called me."

Who the fuck threw something through my home?

It angers her more than it surprises and shocks. While her mind plays with the new havoc being wreaked in her life and what she would like to do to Marilyn for causing it, she tears the shirt off her naked body and flings it on the bed. She would languish in the fragrance and soft material flowing against her skin just because they both belong to Blazier, but she is panicking and not aware of anything happening around her. She barely hears him gasp when she bends over and filches a pair of pink lace underwear from his bedcovers then steps into them. Nor does she pay him much mind when he starts to reverse slowly to the door then leaves, closing it quietly behind him as she dons the matching bra.

Jané is more concerned about what Marilyn has done now while she slept peacefully for the first time in six months. Since she discovered Quon's adultery, every one of those days has been the equivalent of those following her parents' death, and she wishes she never discovered anything.

Blissful ignorance is a hell of a lot better than this reality.

When she is fully dressed, sitting on the bed, and tying her shoes, Blazier returns. Only then does she recall undressing then redressing in front of him without a second thought.

Ah shit!

She did not want him affected by more glimpses of her body when he is not ready to go all the way with her yet. As much as she would love to feel him inside her, she wants to respect his space like he has her vows, much more than she has. She wants to feel guilty about not respecting them, but does not. She gets to her feet then lays an apologetic expression on his face then sees the smile toying with his lips.

Hell, he does not seem to be affected by anything.

Jané decides that mentioning her indiscretion would only make things awkward between them. She does not want that either so she concentrates on the problems weighing her mind down, like how to protect her home from Quon's lover. Hopefully, Blazier does not remember she undressed in front of him nor will she ever remind him of it.

"Ready?" he asks. She nods and grabs her purse. He gets a tender grip on her elbow and guides her at a fast clip through the confusing hallways to the opened front door. They stop at the side of a black Ferrari. Her eyes blink rapidly when he opens the passenger's door of the low slung status symbol. She concludes that the car probably has the same mouth dropping effect when it is wrapped around his body as the swastika does.

"You like symbols, don't you?" she asks dryly. He snickers then guides her inside the car. She decides to not ask why he is not at work, or inquire about his collection of vehicles. None of that seems to be important when she does not even know what time it is, and what he likes and owns is none of her business.

Neither does she complain when he revs the engine then takes off like a bat out of hell through his front gate, cutting the time to her house in half. When it comes into view, she gasps. Three police cars are parked in her drive as the house alarm blares all the way down the street, but she expects that when it is working properly. What she did not anticipate is the gaping hole in her bay window over her favorite rocking chairs.

Blazier parks in the same spot his moving truck occupied yesterday. Jané prepares to shove his door open and leap out of the car. He grabs her arm first and holds her in place. She glares back at him until she understands that he wants her to wait until *he* opens his door. She starts to sputter angrily but nothing comes out.

"Calm down, Jané. What happened here has already happened and you need to be alert before you go inside," he reasons. She gets his point then takes the time to collect herself before he reaches her side of the car. He slides his hands beneath her arms and lifts her out as if she is a baby and sets her on her feet. The officers standing around wait for them to cross the front lawn before one breaks from the group and asks who they are.

Jané tells him she lives here with her husband. He smirks. She gets the notion that he knows exactly who she is talking about, and knows Blazier is not that person. But it does not make a difference if he does because she needs to get inside the home and turn off the sound bringing every neighbor on the block out of their homes.

She quickly pulls her house keys from her purse, unlocks the door, and damn near breaks into a run to cover the few inches to the control panel on the connecting wall. She cannot enter the code and shut down the main attraction for the neighborhood fast enough. Never has she been so completely embarrassed and upset. The cops have never been at her home before now. Two days straight should be more than enough to make up for that, though there seems to be no end in sight of the things Marilyn will do to get her point across.

This bitch has to know Quon's belongings have been shipped to the office by now, that he's locked up, and no longer with me. So, why is she still determined to tear my home and my life apart?

Jané makes a resolution to get to the bottom of Marilyn's rampage and fast, before things escalates, and she is defending her home and her life.

The cops swarm the living area while she disables the alarm. A stout man with a bald head and ill-fitting uniform unlike the other trim officers stops at her side.

"Ma'am, we need you to wait outside while we look for anything out of the ordinary then we'll have you come back in and look for the same as well as anything missing."

She nods as her mind races through possibilities to catch her harasser in the act and get her jailed, or at least acquire enough evidence to get a restraining order. An arm circles her waist. She recognizes who it belongs to then turns into Blazier's body, wraps her arms tightly around his waist, and buries her head in his chest. He leads her onto the front porch. But she is not hiding inside his protective arms this time, just absorbing the comfort of knowing she is not going through all of this alone. Then, a yell erupts from the street.

"What the hell are you doing, Blazier? I allowed you to take care of my wife not *touch* her!"

Oh damn! Who let Quon out of jail?

Chapter Eleven

Jané jumps out from Blazier's hold, feeling guilty instantly, and ponders why she should. Nor does she want to deal with Quon's switches between Dr. Jekyll and Mr. Hyde right now; though she would love to be in Blazier's bed, enjoying the sunlight flooding every inch of the room, giving her a sense of peace and all is right with the world.

Instead, I have that damn hole in my window bugging me and Quon walking up on me like he is about to do something. It's a good thing Blazier is here or I don't know what I'd do about either.

What Jané does know is that she needs for Quon to pipe down about the other man being the only thing she can hold on to in this storm raging around her, which is not her fault.

Blazier steps in front of her. Jané steps to the side of his body again, or rather on the frontlines, preparing for war with whichever Quon that just showed up. When he gets within striking distance, she holds up her palm as Blazier looks down at her curiously.

"Stop right there, Quon, or I swear I'll leave right now and never come back to this hell of your making," she warns in a loud, firm voice with every intention of keeping her promise. She is beyond tired of his split personalities and Marilyn's dangerous one.

Quon stops inches away from her hand.

"Jané, I'm—"

"Didn't I say *stop*, Quon? I don't want to hear anything from you unless I'm talking *to* you. Other than that, shut up. If you say anything to Blazier, breathe on him, or get too close to him, I'm gone. Got it?" Jané realizes she is so far past fed up with her husband, she could actually hit him. But that would be the worst thing to do in front of the police, so she keeps her violent urge in a strangle hold, barely.

Quon nods then eyeballs Blazier with a glare meant to intimidate. Blazier laughs but keeps his eyes on Quon. Jané figures that Blazier can handle himself better than she can and turns her back on both men to stare into the house. Her mind becomes unquiet again, wondering what is bothering her about the broken window.

Why do I feel like I should have seen this coming?

One of the officers disconnects from the crowd scouring her house for evidence that is probably not there. She watches him move toward the front entrance with a medium-sized rock in his hand that would have seriously hurt or killed someone if they had been in the house. It is the same man that asked her to step outside, now stopping in front of her. Jané discerns that the small boulder came from her front lawn. It should be decorating the bottom of the shrubbery, not being presented to her with red letters painted across the flat surface of it. She knows it is another damn message.

"What does it say?" she asks the officer but her eyes refuse to leave the object in his hands. He shifts his generous weight, seeming uneasy about reading it out loud.

"Bitch, this is your last warning. Leave Quon or else."

Jané begins to pivots on her heels slowly, looking for the reason of the message. When her snapping orbs fall on Quon, he is looking like his last meal is about to make a sudden appearance.

In her peripheral, Blazier moves closer to the officer.

"When can she get her stuff? She is not staying here any longer than it takes her to pack it," he announces adamantly.

Before the man can respond, Quon goes from sickly to furious before Jané's eyes.

"She is not leaving this house for another night with you. I know you want my wife, Blazier."

Jané rolls her eyes.

Here we go again.

She turns sideways between the two men.

"Quon *and* Blazier, I decided where I'm going or *if* I'm going. And if you both don't stop, I'll leave you at this house to be Marilyn's next targets."

Quon's mouth drops. His eyebrows lift, clearly taken about by Jané's stand. Before now she never had to reason to take one.

"But, sweetheart—"

"Shut it, Quon. If you think I'm staying here like a sitting duck, you really have lost your mind. Nor do you love me if you'll risk me getting hurt so you can keep up with me. That's done. You've ruined it."

She turns back to the officer.

"I do need to get some more of my things." It nearly breaks her heart to leave her home but she does not want anything hitting her either. She will just have to catch Marilyn in her next criminal act from somewhere else.

Before the officer can reply, Jané is seized by the shoulder and turned around, to face Blazier wearing a look of frustrated concern.

"Where will you go?"

She has no idea. That is one of the many things she has not thought all the way through. She just knows she cannot stay here, not as long as Marilyn has an obsession with destroying everything at this house.

But it is time to fight back.

Jané's mind toys with the idea of getting a weapon, and launching her own projectiles if she has to. But first she needs an address.

"I don't know yet, Blazier, and I'm not risking you being in Marilyn's path. But I do need a car and phone and probably a gun."

Quon gasps.

"What? I can protect you, Jané. You—" He shuts up when she twirls angrily on him.

"No, Quon!" she yells, losing a little more of her grasp on her violent urge to smack his ass. "Why would I stay anywhere near the reason she is doing all this? I want to actually survive this craziness."

He drops his head. For the first time since they met, he seems defeated and weary. Jané would normally address any distress he has before it got this far because she never wanted him to have any. But, her life could be on the line this time and he does not seem all that concerned about that. So, she will take care of herself first this time.

Quon lifts his head again and spears Jané's face with a determined look she has not seen since he started Sullivan's Global.

"Okay, sweetheart. What do you need?" he asks gruffly as if it hurts him to speak. She can hardly believe that Quon has asked. It did not seem like he cared about what she needed anymore.

When she fails to answer, he moves up a step and takes her hands in his.

"If you want to go with Blazier because you feel safer with him, then I understand. God knows I don't want you to go because I can feel the attraction between you two. But I allowed that to happen when I created this mess and I *will* fix it, just don't forget about me." His selfless plea is enough to bring Jané to tears, but she resists the urge to break down in front of so many people. She glances at the neighbors collecting curbside. There is even a gray luxury car creeping by, trying to get a good look at the melee. Jané becomes self-conscious.

I think I will figure out where I'm going on the drive away from here. The whole fucking world seems to be watching.

She releases Quon's hands and swivels to the cop still holding the rock.

"Officer, how long will I have to wait to go upstairs?" She knows she has not answered any of the men's questions but she does not have any answers.

The man in front of her scans Quon's and Blazier's face, probably waiting for them to interrupt like they did each time the officer tried to speak. When no interference comes, his beady eyes lands on Jané's face.

"Right now, we need you to look around downstairs then upstairs before you can pack. We have not seen signs of anything else broken besides the window, but only you can tell us that for sure. We can start now if you like." Jané likes and does not waste time stepping closer to the cop so he knows it, too. He waddles around in a circle then into the house with her, Quon, and Blazier following like stray puppies.

After examining their furniture, neither Jané nor Quon find anything else out of place besides the broken window and scratches on the dark wood frame of the coffee table, indicating the rock bounced across it like someone had skipped it across a river. She still cannot settle the uneasy feeling this incident is not a random occurrence. However, she cannot think clearly with so many people around. Quon and Blazier shadowing her into every room that she enters, is not helping either.

They finally move to upstairs. She looks around thoroughly before telling the officer everything is in its place. He tells her she can start packing now since they are sure burglary has not occurred. Jané stands in the middle of the bedroom and accepts that her stay away from here may be indefinite.

Who knows how long it will take that bitch to get caught?

But it is inevitable.

The angrier Marilyn gets, the sloppier she will get.

Jané glances around the room for what feels like the last time. Then, she makes up her mind to pack now, be sad about it later. On her way to the closet, she spies her cell on the table beside the bed. She veers toward to the nightstand to check the phone for messages, hoping Simone left one, and drops her purse down on it.

In the closet, she finds what she is looking for, a test from her friend. It reads, 'okay' simply, too simply for Jané, or Simone. She wonders why Simone's fiery temper did not make for a lengthier message after she explained why she had to stand her up last night.

Damn, our night out became a no-go and now there really is a rock through my window.

It takes only a second for the coincidence to register in Jané's mind and make her blood run cold.

Simone does not make threats but promises.

Jané stops in the middle of the closet and sinks down to the floor on her knees. Disbelief and despair resound through her head and chest like dull blades, the beginnings of a headache and heartache.

I told her that my car was damaged and Quon was in jail for attacking the cops. If she was a real friend, she would have checked to see if I was okay. Is missing one night at a lounge a reason to break my fucking window and threaten me about Quon?

She knew Simone could get extremely violent when her anger is at an all time high, but Jané never thought her best friend would do something like this to her because of events she had no control over. They have loved each like sisters for four years, and are supposed to be better than this. What hurts the most is that Simone threatened her about Quon. Simone has never had the warm and fuzzies for him.

So what the hell else has changed besides Simone and Quon? Nothing makes sense anymore to Jané, except Simone always has, until now.

Could my best friend really want my husband? Has he been cheating with her, too? No, he wouldn't do…

Jané's mind grinds to a halt and refuses to go any further.

She does not know what Quon will and will not do anymore. He could have very well violated the sanctity of her friendship with Simone though he knows how Jané feels about her. Neither can Jané think of a single reason why Simone or any other woman would not seize the opportunity to have Quon. He is an extraordinary breed of man that is successful, black, handsome, and a cut above the rest when it comes to sex.

"Oh God no," she cries out then covers her mouth.

Blazier rushes into the closet as new waves of rage join her present misery and pain. But, she has to know did Quon take something else from her, Simone, before she walks away from him and never looks back.

"What is it, Jané?" Blazier asks before kneeling beside her. Quon's presence enters the room next. She can always sense when he shows up even when her back is turned. He swallows the air in the room every single time. She figures that will not change, and glad that something will stay the same even if it is to her heart's detriment. If there are any more changes in her world, she will lose her mind completely. Yet, she still has to face the one thing that may be the last straw for her, another betrayal on Quon's end of the marriage.

She points to him without looking up.

"Blazier, I need to speak to Quon privately."

Quon's exhales like he does not want to be a part of the conversation about to take place even when he does not know what may be said. However, if Jané's hunch is right and Quon tells her the truth, she has *two* crazy bitches sending her messages about a man that is no longer hers.

As if one crazy bitch is not one too fucking many already.

Blazier stands up and strolls out the room quickly then closes the door behind him. Quon walks further in slowly like he is cautious about his family jewels again. Jané does not bother to get off her knees. If he confirms her suspicions, she will drop right back down to them anyway.

He crouches down beside her. She cannot seem to lift her eyes off the floor. She is already feeling the weight of a relationship gone down the tubes because of Quon before she even gets to his parents, and cannot bear to look at him.

She takes the deepest breath she can before saying, "Quon." His name is only a whisper on her lips.

"Yeah, sweetheart," he answers worriedly. He should be worried, because Jané does not know what will happen next when he says he is responsible for Simone going off the rails, too.

"I'm going to ask you something and I need the truth. You have to promise to tell me everything," she begs softly then realizes what she is doing and where she is doing it.

It took him one hundred and eighty-five days but he finally brought me to my knees and I'm still begging him. But I don't know if I will ever stand up again after this.

He takes a seat beside Jané.

"Okay, baby…I'll tell you everything! Now what is it?" The anxiety in his tone grows with each word.

"Promise you'll tell me the truth, Quon. No more secrets."

"I promise! Just ask," he insists in a thunderous tone, drawing her attention. He looks like he is about to jump out of his skin. She does not feel compassionate toward him in the least. How can she when he will not stop breaking her heart?

Still, she gathers the courage to ask him to break her heart one more time.

"Did you sleep with Simone?"

His eyes try to jump out of his head.

"Hell no! I can't *stand* that girl and I do have standards and limits even after all the cheating I have done. She may have the foulest mouth in the state but she is your best friend. Why would you even ask me that? Better yet, don't answer that." Quon chuckles at his own bad joke.

Jané wishes she could simply smile. Even though his betrayals seem to have stopped piling up, she still has to get over her heartache from losing her closest friend whose betrayals are starting to rise, and then tell Quon *why* she has lost Simone.

"Simone is the one that broke our window," she confesses quietly. Quon may think he has dodged a bullet because he is not guilty of something this time, but Simone and Marilyn are still free to plan their next attack on them. Simone may be the worst of the two.

He stops smiling.

"Why in the hell would she do that?"

Jané turns to give Quon *her* pity for once.

"Because…Simone wants you…and it's my fault."

Text ROYALTY to 42828 to keep up

with our new releases!

Looking for a publishing home?

Royalty Publishing House, Where the Royals reside, is accepting submissions for writers in the urban fiction genre. If you're interested, submit the first 3-4 chapters with your synopsis to submissions@royaltypublishinghouse.com. Check out our website for more information: www.royaltypublishinghouse.com.

Be sure to <u>LIKE</u> our Royalty Publishing House
page on Facebook

Made in the USA
Charleston, SC
08 June 2016